MURTAIREAN
AN ASSASSIN'S TALE

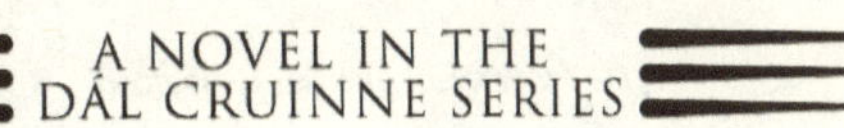

A NOVEL IN THE
DÁL CRUINNE SERIES

JENN LEES

Cover by Fiona Jayde Media

www.fionajaydemedia.com

This novel is written in British English.

Murtairean is the Gaelic word for assassins.

Contents

ONE

Vygeas drew a sigh from deep within and stretched his legs in the small cell. His boot connected with the iron door, filling the confined space with a metallic rattle that vibrated and tunnelled into his hearing.

"Guard. Guard!" The gravelly voice of the poor sod in the next cell rang in his ears and had done so since they threw the man beside Vygeas in the cart that had brought them back to Lord Ciarán's dungeon in chains. "This 'ere slop bucket shud hae been emptied twa days ago, aye?" His fellow prisoner addressed the question to him.

Vygeas grimaced. His cellmates used the far corner now and his acute awareness was a curse under these circumstances. His nose burned with the ammonia from the turned urine wafting into his nostrils, but it was nothing compared to the scorch of fear reeking off his fellow prisoners.

"Deserters all, we are." The man pressed his face against the bars between their two small cells. "The hangman's noose for us," the scrap of humanity beside Vygeas sighed. "Or maybe a sharp blade against our necks. That would be merciful."

He wouldn't get that. It *was* Lord Ciarán to whom Vygeas had sold his sword... and turned his back. Five solid years of service meant nothing to that lord.

I only wanted to be a warrior.

But Lord Ciarán had noted his skill. Singled him out. Promised him a more interesting life.

Aye, working as a lone assassin had agreed with him. None to question his past. Enquire as to how he fought like he did. How he knew what would happen next... what was around the nearest corner... what the enemy would do before it was apparent.

Stealth and the skills of death had come easily. The side of his mouth pulled tight in chagrin for they had come *too* easily.

Constant comments and whimpers hit his ears and the sharp faecal scent of fear came in waves from this farmer turned soldier in the next cell.

Some people never cease the chatter and the wretch's pitch had risen with every utterance.

Vygeas' forehead tightened, and he danced his fingers on his thigh.

Blades and bows! He could not blame his overloaded senses and exhaustion for his capture. It was his own utter stupidity that landed him here.

He should have run! But no. His warband companions had scoured the village and would not stop at his pleas. Women and wee ones scurried, and chickens scattered while war horses spurred by their riders mowed them down. Small broken bodies lay in the mud-churned road, the path itself dotted by wailing women cradling crumpled forms.

Enough! He pressed the heels of his palms into his eyes against the memory, chains rattling at his cuffs. *Cease!*

He'd struck down two of Lord Ciarán's warriors in the act of chasing those villagers who'd fled. He reached behind and touched the bump on the back of his skull then winced. Aye, the other warriors had not been gentle, turning on him in unison. He'd woken up, bleary eyed with a massive headache, to find himself restrained in the back of a rattling cart.

Hardened leather shoes clumped on the sandstone steps and echoed down the circular stairwell. The scrape of a wooden torch-pole travelling along the curving cut-stone wall accompanied the footsteps increasing in intensity. The burning torch illuminated the surroundings and prisoners in the other chambers stirred. The light revealed what he perceived without its aid—dirty straw, ragged breeches and leather armour, lice infested companions, and a guard who couldn't care less.

The guard directed his cockiness at Vygeas as the cast-iron key clunked into the heavy lock and clanked its turning.

"Out." The guard's curtness was no surprise. "The lord and master wishes to see ye."

Vygeas' stood, his muscles screaming after days of inactivity cramped in the tiny cell. He ambled out, his grey coat trailing in the muck, holding his breath against the sour vomit-like odour emitted from the guard's mouth. He'd detected it from his cell and now must walk right past it.

He raised his face to the cool breeze swirling down the stairwell and sucked in its freshness. The guard led him up the stone stairs, the sandstone glowing a dusky yellow in the burning torchlight.

Out of the cell—*at last!* Days of incarceration made one think on life—and death.

He held tight to memories of his father, a peasant farmer with no aspirations other than to survive. A man who had never understood his son's desire for something more.

To live for combat. To fight and finally feel truly alive. Muscles solid, healthy and strong. His blood pounding around his body. The weapons in his grasp a very part of his being. Skills honed till he wielded them with accuracy.

Ah... the beauty of the blade. The wondrous joy of battle.

He sighed. *Da never understood.*

There was another memory he could never escape.

Holding his love in his arms—his dead love. He pushed it down.

Nothing could change *that* now.

Forced to do the very act himself, it had burned his soul and left him drifting. Eager for forgiveness—but there was none alive who could bestow it—and eager for his soul's repair.

He snorted. So far, he had not found it.

Lord Ciarán's kill orders for that village had reawakened this need. Now he could not, *would not*, do it...kill innocents and torture his soul all over again.

I do not wish to be that man anymore...risk that callous murderer raising his head.

Perhaps it was evil enough that he did kill under orders, but only ever those who deserved it. The truly wicked selfish ones of this world who cared naught for those they destroyed on their path to their ambition's fulfillment.

Lord Ciarán had a never-ending list of such as those...or so it seemed.

The tower's exit brought him into a courtyard. He flinched against the daylight and lifted his arms to shade his eyes, chains clattering. The guard's vice-like grip encircled his upper-arm, digging a band of pain as an armlet, while he marched Vygeas across the flagstone-paved yard to the opposite door leading to Lord Ciarán's Great Hall where he performed his lordly obligations.

It would be official then.

So be it.

Vygeas' insides coiled. It was not Lord Ciarán's custom to deal gently—with anyone.

He pressed his lips around a curse and ground his teeth. Noble sentiments had brought him to this place. Desertion—and escape—would have been his opportunity to make a fresh start.

No, his aching desire for a turning in his soul, a change in direction of his life's path, had led to this *now*. In that very cell facing a very real hanging.

No chance of reforming with death near. It was too late a repentance.

Vygeas reached the tower entrance and the guard shoved him through to where Lord Ciarán awaited. Sunlight streamed in long oblong blocks onto the hardwood floor of the Great Hall of this fortress. A fire raged in a stone fireplace large enough to fit the living quarters of the steading house in which he had spent his formative years.

Lord Ciarán stood before it; a tall, greying man with a clear mind and sharp tongue. The early singe of the lord's clothes hit Vygeas' heightened sense of smell.

Lord Ciarán narrowed his eyes on spying Vygeas' entrance.

"Thought you could turn on your own and remain unpunished?" Pleased anger radiated from the nobleman and hit him like a crimson wall along with the heat of the flames.

Vygeas halted before Lord Ciarán.

"You're a good assassin but a poor warrior, boy." The lord's growl vibrated out of his throat. "You deserve death by hanging."

Vygeas remained firm against the crimson waves coming from Lord Ciarán. Golden pleasure streaked these waves and surely he would discover its source any moment now.

"Nothing to say for yourself?" Lord Ciarán's chest rose and fell in a steady motion.

Vygeas swallowed. Silence was the best option when Lord Ciarán was in a mood such as this.

"Want to live, do you?" The man's glare held firm.

"Aye." Vygeas' hoarse words came through a dry throat.

"I'm in a magnanimous mood." Lord Ciarán's hands jiggled behind his back. "You're fortunate, for as you know, that is a rare occurrence."

Vygeas stood taller. Out of the corner of his eye, he glimpsed a sage entering the Great Hall. He was one of the wise masters in their fields of knowledge who advised and provided tutelage to the nobility and privileged landowners. The swish of the sage's black hooded-robe accompanied his passage across to his lord, black cloth signifying the man's status as a mage. A red vapour, verging on violet, oozed from this man's very core.

Anticipation mixed with...?

The mage gave Lord Ciarán a scroll then turned to Vygeas.

Vygeas' heart, which for these past few days had seemed silent in his chest, leaped into his throat and pounded as a smile encompassed the mage's face.

"Greetings, Vygeas." The mage's smile was self-satisfied.

"Drostan." Vygeas breathed his composure back to normal.

"Ah, you know him, Drostan?" A barely restrained smirk twitched Lord Ciarán's mouth and deception's malodour wafted from him.

"Aye, I have had dealings with the lad in the past." Drostan slid his gaze away from Vygeas as if he were of little consequence. "All you need is there, my lord." He pointed to the scroll Lord Ciarán held, then stood back, taking his place beside his master.

Grasping the chains that dangled from his wrist irons, Vygeas clenched his fists. How could Drostan remain alive? How many other young men had he deceived with his evil ways? How many women lost? Elyse's golden hair was once more soft silken strands sliding through his fingers—

"I have a job for you, Vygeas." Lord Ciarán pointed the scroll at him.

Vygeas snapped back to the Great Hall where the lord's steel grey eyes pierced him. "A job, my lord?"

"Aye. Your forté. A contract on a mark." Lord Ciarán locked his gaze. "Do this and you avoid the gallows."

Vygeas double blinked, his brow remaining tight, then his heart again reminded him of its presence, skipping a beat.

Is this a ruse?

"I've heard you have to justify the death of your victims. Eases your guilt somewhat, I believe." Lord Ciarán paused and sneered. "A merchant in Eilean isn't cooperating. Gille Fhialain. I need him to be an example to others. Access to the trading routes to which the island clings is vital for my army's supplies. That salve from the east accelerates healing and will return my warriors to the field in short time." He leaned closer, the aroma of smoked salmon wafting into Vygeas' face. "Do it. Prove it, and you are free."

The prospect of life and liberty tasted sweet as Vygeas' guts complained at the lack of food, but the back of his neck prickled and the rusted manacles around his wrists dug in. He surely had nae choice. Lord Ciarán held Vygeas' life, and his obedience ensured he took his next breath.

"Aye, my lord."

He would not trust every word that passed Lord Ciarán's lips. But perhaps freedom did truly await—a chance to escape this lord's cell and his own death. And rid himself of Lord Ciarán's hold over him and be at last a free man.

The lord snapped his fingers in dismissal and for a second Vygeas landed his gaze on the mage. Deep crimson edged his own sight, gusting from his peripheral vision, it rose like a shield wall matching the wall of Lord's Ciarán's anger that had slammed into him on his entry to this hall.

Drostan...Blades and Bows, it wasn't over. Now he knew where the mage was.

Drostan's dark eyes held steady with his, a slow curve turning up his mouth.

But will I be able to snuff this one who certainly deserves *it?*

And would he lose his gift if he did succeed? The advantage wrought by the man's magic so long ago?

He snatched his eyes from Drostan's overconfident glare, nodded a bow, and walked toward the Great Hall's main doors.

He squinted, for he would pursue this task of Lord Ciarán's with watchfulness.

"Guard," Lord Ciarán's voice rang in the hall behind him, "I'm feeling generous today. Remove the sell-sword's chains and feed him. Restore to him his weapons and his horse."

"Aye, my lord," the guard grunted.

"And Vygeas." Lord Ciarán spoke to his back.

Tightness raced across his shoulders. *There is always a catch.*

Vygeas turned. "Aye, my lord?"

"This merchant, Gille Fhialain, plans to soon sail to the east on an extended trip to gather wares."

Eilean...if he recalled correctly, that was four day's ride from here.

"But—?"

The hue on Lord Ciarán face coincided with a welling rage of dusky crimson emanating from him, shutting Vygeas' mouth on his protest.

"Aye, my lord." He should expect no less.

Vygeas bowed and exited the hall, making his way to the smithy and freedom.

Freedom from his chains at least.

Two

A Tavern in Dál Gallain

Pungent aromas of malt and stale beer hit Leyna's nostrils. The tavern's sign dangled from a rusted bracket and paint peeled off the picture of the fabled red beast from which the *Flying Dragon* derived its name. Chips dented the wattle-and-daube structure, and the entrance door hung partially off its hinges. Leyna sighed and her stomach answered with a grumble. A tavern was food and warmth for a time, no matter the state of its exterior. She pulled up the collar of her jacket, trusting it would continue to hide the leather armour she wore underneath, tugged her cap over her brow, and prayed that once again she would be taken for a lad. It had worked thus far since leaving Robbie and the band.

Robbie... She let the air escape her lungs in a silent sigh.

The door creaked open and a man with silvery hair and a weather-beaten face staggered out, a cane supporting his willowy frame. A woman held the door open, her mob-cap sitting askew, and grease stains dotting the apron covering her long skirts.

"Aye, lad?" The landlady of the establishment directed her harsh voice at Leyna and glanced at her breeches. "There's a spare seat at the long bench by the fire. Ye look like ye require warming up, son. Come in with ye." She inclined her head, her words themselves friendlier than her tone.

Leyna entered the tavern. The interior was a room of moderate size and lamplit, with long wooden tables and bench seats arranged centrally. Candles burned in sconces placed along the walls above the booth-seating at the edges of the room. Smoke from the open fireplace hung low in the air, mingling with the scent of ale, tobacco-sticks and unwashed bodies.

"Over there, laddie." The woman's face was close to Leyna's ear. "We've added more tables due to the likes of yoursel' travelling away from the troubles."

Leyna tipped her head to avoid shouting over the noise and give away the fact that she was *not* a lad.

Patrons called to the serving women for more food and drink. The echo of clanking pots and loud commands accompanied the aroma of food coming from the galley kitchen. Leyna sniffed. It was the gentle smell of a stew of some sort, without the strong aroma of meat. Her stomach growled, and she placed her hand over her belly to contain the hunger-pain there.

"Cheat!" a man yelled as Leyna walked past a booth and she stifled a flinch. The man pointed his dirt-ingrained finger to his companion sitting opposite him. Playing cards fanned on the cracked and knotted tabletop before them and coins sat scattered among crusts of bread. Leyna turned from the ensuing argument and strode on to the place at the bench seat nearest the fire then sat between two middle-aged women who tucked their skirts around them to make space for her.

Leyna sat with the grate of hot coals behind her and soon heat seeped through her jacket and leather chest armour. A serving maid in a mob-cap, with hair tucked neatly beneath, thrust a wooden bowl of stew before her. The bowl landed on the table, sloshing potatoes and carrots in a brown liquid.

"Coin first." She held out her hand.

Leyna pulled out the coin-pouch on her belt and placed three copper pieces in the serving maid's open palm, then turned back to her meal.

"Ya needn't stare so hard, lad. Dinnae expect meat, aye? All oor beasts have gone tae war, ken? Tae feed thems that fight." The serving maid leaned in closer. "*And* all oor young men."

Leyna lifted her shoulder against the woman's breath in her ear, pulled her spoon from her jacket and dipped it into the watery stew.

Laughter came from the women who were the only occupants of the far corner booth. Men and women in travel-worn clothing sat at the long trestle tables, some with youngsters who sat quietly or, like herself, spooned in their meal. Men, middle-aged and older, sat in the booths, eating and drinking. Their conversation hummed through the room, interspersed with loud exclamations that echoed off the walls. They wore leather vests over loose linen shirts and warm breeches of sturdy material. They were locals, relaxed in their usual gathering place, no doubt, but their serious faces held grim expressions.

"Lord Ciarán demands it." One man's deep voice rumbled over to her. "Our taxes are funding his battles." He squinted into his tankard.

"Aye, and payin' fer it wi' oor youngsters," an elderly man seated with him retorted. "Too ambitious, is that lord. Wants the high kingship, I'll wager. It'll be all oot war afore we know it."

"Bleeding us dry in the process." The deep-spoken man cocked his head and then lifted his tankard and drained it.

Five men sat in the booth beside the fire to Leyna's right. The young, sturdy, and well-armed men wore leather coats, with weapons at their belts and backs, observing all in the room. Perhaps they were folk of her own ilk.

"*Murtairean.*" A serving maid muttered under her breath as she stepped past, her upper lip twisted in a snarl.

That confirmed it. Assassins, then.

Their low-voiced discussion drifted over to her.

"'Ow much did 'e say?" one asked.

"Enough to buy us that seaworthy rig." The bald head of the speaker shone in the light of the sconces.

"Don't forget,"—a woman's voice came from deep within the booth— "all the wealth belonging to that merchant goes to the successful one."

Leyna blinked, still spooning her stew, feigning disinterest. Their talk was familiar. Probably a *hit*. If only she could discover where.

"Yeah, but Eilean's gonna be mobbed with assassins, ain it? Now Lord Ciarán's put the word out—" A harsh chorus of curses from his companions interrupted the first speaker.

"What? Ain't nobody 'ere gonna know what I mean. Probably don't even know who Gille Fhialain is, hey?"

"Silence, you fool," the woman's voice snapped.

The sea rover leaned into his companions, a small silver hoop dangling from his ear. "As if we need *his* permission to take that merchant's wealth!"

Leyna spooned the last of her meal as the discussion moved on to the brewing war. It seemed this Lord Ciarán caused much that was not good.

Leyna smiled to the women seated beside her, stood, and walked to the galley door, where she bought a small hunk of dried venison wrapped in a cloth. For a price. She grimaced. Her purse was now much lighter. Stowing the meat in her bag, she stepped past patrons and made her way out, leaving the chatter, tobacco-stick smoke, and heat behind her. The landlady opened the door to the cobbled road.

"Och, I've seen ye have paid." She spoke over Leyna's head in a gruff voice. "Where would ye be off to tha noo'? No' going anywhere near those skirmishes, lad? A youngin' like yourself shud nae be involved in a war. Leave that for those older and stupider than you, aye?" The landlady waited for an answer.

"I was thinking I'd head to the coast, to the Isle of Eilean." Leyna deepened her voice to speak. "I hear there is a merchant there, Gille Fhialain."

"Och lad, you dinnae want tae work for him. He does nae pay his workers. They're starvin' while he and his chubby wifey live in luxury. Or so they say. There're plenty other merchants on that isle. Ye try another, ken?" She finished with a nod then banged the door closed behind her.

Leyna turned eastward, striding away from the tavern and all its talk. She needed a place to sleep in safety this night. She slipped her hand through her jacket and gipped the handle of her short sword. The trouble was closer than ever before on her journey. But the news of the mark set by Lord Ciarán... The man's name was spoken often of late. She held no love for this lord, but his game, so to speak, would be her vindication.

Gold wasn't her reward. Nor her goal. She would head to the Isle of Eilean in search of satisfaction. Assassins gathered, soon to crowd the island, and her parents' killer would most assuredly be there. Maybe even one of those she'd observed in the tavern. The confined space full of eager ears was not the place to enquire, nor the place to act.

Her chest tightened, so did her grasp on her sword. The opportunity on Eilean would be the closest thing to a chance she would ever have. She hadn't turned her back on home, lands, and title, perfected her martial art, and kept company with thieves for the love of it.

No, revenge burned within her, and she would have it find its target.

THREE

A Village Near Lord Ciarán's Tower

The semi-charred odour of oatmeal tickled Aiden's nose, waking him from slumber. Nan stooped over the cooking pot hanging from the hook above the coals, stirring the morning meal with an iron spoon in one hand and holding her worn skirts away from the fire with the other. Aiden rolled over on his sleeping mat by the hearth, his legs nudging Bessie who still slept. Pop's bed was empty.

"Aye, lazy lump. Your pop is oot gathering the peat ye cut. It'll be dry tha noo." Nan leaned over him, the skin on her usually plump face sagged at her jowls. "Up ye get."

Aiden stretched and rubbed the soft hair coming on his chin. He stood. The pan Nan stirred was only half full.

Nan and Pop would have enough to eat if it weren't for him and Bessie.

"I'll go out and help plant the spelt today." He took hold of the wooden bowl Nan had filled with oat gruel, but she held it firm.

"Ye need to find work that will bring coin into the house, lad." Nan's crinkled brow deepened with her words. "We hav' tae pay the rent. Still owin' frae last month, ken?"

Aiden blinked and she released the bowl from her grip. He stood to break his fast, leaving the only chair for Nan.

"Nan?" He spooned the gruel in then swallowed as she looked up from her half-full bowl. "Where around here will I find paid work?" His throat tightened as her words' true meaning hit him.

"Aye." Her grey head bobbed gently. "Ye'll have tae leave us, mayhap. But we'll no make it without some income. We can just feed ourselves from what we grow but the lord's taxes..." She shook her head, gazing into the fire.

Aiden followed her stare to the glowing red coals. He would do as asked. Mam wouldn't wish to know her parents were now worse off because she was no longer with them. Aiden let the numbness linger, but only for a moment.

"I can be a smithy."

"With what, lad?" Nan's face softened but her words were sharp. "Ye have nae forge. It went payin' the debt your faither left when he died."

"But I ken what tae do. I watched Da." He could do it. He was sure of it. And he had the skill to place a shoe on a hoof. So, he could be a farrier too.

Nan stood and set her hand on her hip. "Whatever ye find, I ken ye'll do well, Aiden. Ye are a good lad. Promise me ye'll stay that way, aye?"

Aiden straightened his shoulders. The cap on Nan's head needed mending. His mouth twitched. He was taller than her now. Much taller.

"Aye, Nan. I promised Mam I would."

A half smile came to her lips for a second, then her usual stern expression found its way back to her face. "On ye go, then. That's yoor day's task, lad."

Outside, a horse nickered.

Pebbles ground against the tender arches of Leyna's feet and she flinched as yet another stabbing stone broke through the soles of her worn leather boots. Oh, how she missed a horse. But she wouldn't complain. She'd escaped with her life—found the way out, as usual.

She straightened her shoulders, walking taller. Of all the tricks the band of thieves had taught her, her own natural skill at finding the quickest way out had been her salvation.

But not theirs.

She lowered her eyes to the pebbled path before her while her face heated.

I was smart. Clever. They should have been too!

I refuse to feel guilty for surviving when they did not.

She had retreated with the scuffles and cries of the band behind her. None had followed. From a ledge near a roof top, she'd spied the caisteal guards manhandling the others.

Including Robbie.

Then they had hung them while she hid among the crowd at a safe distance. Unknown. Her lover's feet had twitched as he wet himself in that final act of humiliation. She'd dragged the tears away from her face with a determined hand and moved on.

I had to.

Three moons had passed, and she had worn out her shoes. She huffed. Traipsing the countryside will do that.

What a magnificent place it was though, and her only solace.

The mighty grey cloud-hugging mountains that edged the green-grassed moors were always a place to go when...

She bit her lip and let out a shaky sigh. Aye, the wild country had consoled her in the past. The place to run when grief had chased.

And she had returned to it on the death of her man.

Her relationship with Robbie had been a joining of convenience, a non-formalised necessity in her situation. In all practicality, an initiation requirement. A must if she were to join the band of thieves...not only join but survive in it.

But a soft ache still sat there.

Leyna sighed and lifted her head. Vivid greens and golden browns lit by the patchy sunshine illuminated the mountainsides surrounding the valley, as pure white clouds skimmed their peaks. She ambled across a wooden bridge over a chattering burn, its rapids white with the swirl of fast-flowing water. Beside her path, grey drystone walls covered in green furry moss lined the way and edged the heather-covered moor.

The road led her past a guarded tower. The sandstone circular fortress was a nobleman's abode, a lord who owned land passed on from generation to generation. She could not recall the current lord of this district. Most of these lords were lesser rulers, as Father had been. After the talk at the tavern last night, she would wager this was the fortification and lands of Lord Ciarán.

She skirted the grounds and buildings near the mound, which was the foundation of the fortified tower. The lord's warriors would guard the tower, stables, and armoury, while his skilled tradesmen and vassals worked in the buildings at its base. The meadows where stock grazed, and the fields sown with crops, were an easier place to hide if warriors rode near.

She would not risk recognition, though she wore no tartan to signify her clan. Nothing could persuade her to return to her lands, title, and inheritance. Abiding by the rules and expectations of society had got her parents killed. It would hold no power over her.

A churning heat returned to her belly, newly rekindled from the assassins' talk in the tavern. Someone would pay for her parents' deaths and the *someone* was sure to be on that island. All the skills Robbie had taught her would *not* go to waste.

Leyna passed the round tower and now the purple heather-carpeted slopes she walked directed her gaze to a small village nestled at the base of a gentle hill.

She limped to the whitewashed walls and thatched roofs of the cottages at the edge of this quiet hamlet. An old man pushed a wheelbarrow full of dried peat down the cobbled street, shuffling with each step. His jumper had a hole in the elbow and his cap sat on dirty hair. It was early morning, but no aroma of baking bread came from the cottages. One or two chickens scratched around the dirt by the road. A row of flowers edged the drystone wall of a house near the hamlet's crossroads. She drew closer and gasped at the tiny white perfection of the flowers.

"Greetings, lady." A small girlish voice spoke beside her.

Leyna turned in time to see the child curtsey.

"Oh, I'm not a lady." Leyna held out her hand to stop the girl drawing attention to her.

Surely her worn shoes and leather garb would indicate otherwise?

Definitely not the dress of a lady.

The thin young girl gave a wistful grin and hugged herself. Her collarbones were prominent, and her cheek bones drawn. A tightness struck Leyna's chest. She had worn out her shoes but at least she'd eaten. Leyna rummaged in the bag she'd slung over her shoulder, adjusting its strap as it caught on the handle of her short sword hanging on the belt. She held out the left-over cheese to the child, and the girl grasped it tight.

"You can have it. Take it." Leyna let go.

The girl curtsied once more and ran off to the house where an elderly woman peered out.

Leyna scanned the road. Maybe none else had seen the exchange and especially not the curtsey. The cottages of this small village were tidy but unadorned. Farm workers trudged in the direction Leyna had come, heading to the lands of the lord of the round tower. They were old men and women with not a young man among them. All able-bodied men called upon by their lord to serve in his army, no doubt. Farmers made into warriors.

Vegetables grew in the small gardens, and apart from the tiny white flowers at her feet, no other plants grew for their beauty alone. It seemed hard times had come to this hamlet. From the talk in that tavern last evening, heavy taxes burdened the local people, forced to provide for the warriors sent to fight.

She pressed her teeth onto her bottom lip. She headed for troubled country. No peaceful scenic beauty to surround and comfort her so she would take more care.

At the crossroads of this hamlet, a youth stood next to a tall, well-built man who held the reins of a war horse. The man's long brown hair was in the style of a warrior, hanging down his back but tied away from his face by a leather thong. His freshly shaven face had a shiny chin and cheeks. Over his shoulder stood the handle of a broadsword. His long, grey-hooded coat flipped open in the wind revealing leather chest armour and a dagger at his belt. A scar crossed his right eyebrow, and another pulled down the corner of his mouth. He had seen action and was on his way to join in the battles, no doubt.

The warrior and the youth were in conversation; the man wore a taciturn frown, but the boy spoke with eagerness.

"I ken horses. My Da was the smithy of the village and the farrier too. I helped him, ken?" The lad had that in-between-boy-and-man look about him. He moved as if his limbs had grown but his co-ordination hadn't yet realised.

"I'm on a journey. I'm not quite there—" The man spoke well but not like a nobleman-warrior. There was commoner in his speech, although he hid it well.

"I can come." The lad interrupted him, his brown curls overhanging his face. "I'll tell my nan. She'll be all right about it, ken." His head almost nodded off his neck in his enthusiasm.

Leyna's mouth twitched at the corners.

"But if I employ you," the warrior continued, "you must leave with me." Hesitation laced his voice.

"I'll send my wages back." The lad was insistent, and he approached the massive beast the man held by the reins. Even though the lad was tall the war horse stood way above him, its enormous head dwarfing his. A shiny chestnut coat, long mane, feathering at its fetlocks, sturdy musculature—it was a fine animal.

How did this warrior afford it? There were patches on his coat, mud-splashes on his leather breeches, and his boots were worn. Not as bad as her own, but the heels were low.

War horses had a reputation for meanness, at least those Leyna had known. But the lad had a way with this one. A natural. The horse nickered acceptance.

The lad glanced at the stone cottage; the same one the girl had entered. An elderly woman stared out the door at him.

"No. I'm not—" The warrior's frown creased his forehead as the youth ran toward this cottage and the old woman whom Leyna suspected was 'Nan'.

Leyna manoeuvred behind the wall where she was out of the warrior's sight, but still able to observe.

The warrior rubbed a rough sword-hand over his mouth, but not before an expletive escaped. He dropped his hand; the last two fingers sat curved—common physical defect from holding a sword long and tight. The two straight fingers tapped his thigh. His eyes followed the girl shuffling beside the old woman, clutching her skirts, the same girl to whom Leyna had given the cheese, and now his expression had turned from resignation to understanding.

Leyna nodded to herself, for it was most likely the family was hungry, and the boy would be their means of income.

Decision crossed the warrior's face like a cloud shadow rippling across a moor. He stood taller and a crooked smile, impeded by the scar to his lip, spread a hesitant way across his mouth as the lad made his way back to him.

The warrior mounted his horse and turned the large beast away out of the village. The old woman strode out to the youngster and handed him a small pack of belongings. He took them, then the old woman wrapped him in a tight hug, whispered something in his ear, and walked back to the cottage, never turning. She wiped her face once she reached her door. The lad scurried after the warrior on the horse and waved a cheery goodbye to the young girl.

"Can I help ye, lass?" An old man leaned over the fence. The same man who had pushed the wheelbarrow down the hamlet's street.

"Oh." Leyna straightened. "I'm fine, thank you." She hobbled onto the road out of the village in the same direction as the warrior and boy.

"What size feet are ye?" The old man's heavy accent made her turn back.

"Pardon?"

"What size of boot do ye tak, lassie? I ken yoor feet are hurtin' ye." He nodded to her worn shoes. "It's just that, well, oor own lass died and we have nae need of her shoes nae more, if ye'd wish 'em. I saw ye gave our granddaughter some food, like. In thanks, ken?"

His gentle voice was hard to resist.

"Thank you."

He shuffled back to the cottage and then returned carrying a pair of boots. The heel was solid and there was little sign of wear on the sole. Leyna removed her worn boots and slipped her feet in the boots he handed to her. They fit perfectly.

"I can't tell you how much this means. Thank you again." Her heart warmed at this needy family. Poor materially but not poor in spirit.

"Ye are welcome, lass. I wish ye well on yoor journey." He smiled and tipped his hat in farewell.

Leyna strode out of the hamlet. The shoes were not new, but sturdy and comfortable and the previous owner had broken in the hard leather. Ahead, a thick forest of pine and elm crowded the road either side. The breeze stirred the forest's air and the moist smell of leaf-litter and pine needles swirled in her path. She slipped into the forest edge, the wind singing through the treetops.

If that warrior and his new knave slowed their journey any, she'd bump into them. The warrior had behaved with honour on hiring the lad and shown that a kind heart beat beneath his fierce, scarred exterior. Leyna's lower lip pinched where she'd bit it. A land of unrest wasn't the safest place for a woman travelling alone, even one able to defend herself. She took the throwing knives out of her vest and tucked them into her new boots. She would observe this warrior for some leagues, then decide.

But he was only one man. Maybe a good one. Her mouth skewed to the side. Perhaps goodness *did* still exist in this world.

FOUR

Dräger's hooves *clip clopped* for the first few miles. The only sound.
Utter bliss.

"So, my Da passed away and then my Mam. Nan and Pop are great but, ye ken they cannae work in the fields nae more."

In the edge of Vygeas' vision, the lad, Aiden, peered up at him mounted on his stallion. Soft downy fluff covered the lad's upper lip. He was keen to please.

Too keen.

A niggle prodded Vygeas' relative calm.

"I saw how Da sharpened swords too. I can do that for ye, if ye wish?"

"I hired you to hold my horse and see to him at the end of the day. That will suffice." Vygeas faced the road ahead. His words should silence the lad.

It was a long way to the Isle of Eilean, which sat not far off the south-eastern coast. It was a trading and market island with some small business houses producing goods, and a harbour facing its seaward side. Some said when the tide was out, you could traverse the sands to the island from the shore opposite but many an unwary sand-walker had drowned as the tide surged in like a wall of water.

"You come from the land, do ye not...sir?" Aiden's voice poked into his thoughts.

Vygeas blinked. "What?" Had the lad *not* ceased talking?

"My lord, I hear by your accent ye, well, aren't of noble blood." Aiden smiled.

As if that smile would help.

"I am your master. You are my knave. That will suffice."

"Your accent sounds like ye are from Dál Gaedhle, my lord."

"Blades and bows! I hired ye to hold ma horse, not to chatter."

"Very well." Aiden bowed his head. "Horse holding. No speaking. Got it."

With the ensuing silence, Vygeas sank into the calm of his saddle. Dräger's hooves continued their rhythmic tread, and sunlight broke through the patchy cloud, warming Vygeas' face. Hills surrounded the road—browns splashed with purples and yellows, just like the majestic mountains he had left behind so long ago. The year burst with spring. He must do this job quickly and escape Lord Ciarán's lands before the lord mustered more warbands and raids, blocking any routes north-west.

A sensation prickling between Vygeas' shoulder blades nagged at him. It had followed them since Aiden's wee village. It came from the forest. Forests often did that to him. It could be the animals within or the trees themselves.

His mind flew back to Drostan, now in the employ of Lord Ciarán. When had that occurred? What plans did Lord Ciarán have for that evil mage? His hand gripped the reins tighter. He hadn't seen Drostan since the day the mage had granted him his gift.

The worst and the best day of his life.

Perhaps he would never fully understand how his heightened senses worked. How he knew immediately the sensations that belonged to an emotion—a sharpness, a heat, a particular scent. He had searched his mind, his feelings, and his inner self to discover how this magic worked in him. And now, as always, these enquiring thoughts led him nowhere. He shook his head. Such workings of magic were beyond him.

The rustling of leaves reached his ears. It came from about half a league back. A human mumbled, the words incomprehensible to him at such a distance. Pain floated through the air. Not severe. The person who followed was making heavy work of it. Trying to remain hidden, no doubt. And keeping back.

Frustration wafted up from the lad beside him, tempered with short bursts of the green vapour of calmness. Aiden seemed to find it difficult to keep quiet. Why a talker, of all things? He should have discovered *that* before taking pity and hiring the youngster.

By late afternoon, having covered some decent miles, the boy dragged his feet and his shoulders slumped.

"There is a clearing ahead. We'll camp there. Small fire. Don't want to attract attention. You can light a fire, can ye not, son of a smithy?"

"Aye, and I can trap a rabbit for our dinner. Roast rabbit, done over coals." The lad's mouth ran with salivary juices.

At moments such as these he spurned his gift of enhanced senses. It was an asset in a fight and for his profession as an assassin but...like now, *not one at all.*

Aiden's scrawny neck, and his slim wee sister, were a testament to the scarcity of food in his poor wee village. Vygeas grunted. In all certainty, Lord Ciarán's army had requisitioned their village's produce.

Vygeas pulled up Dräger at the clearing between two copses of ash and elm trees. The grass was thin between them and suitable for making a decent fire. They would need the heat. The air cooled as the silver sun began its descent behind the mountains in the east, chilling his face. He dismounted Dräger and hobbled him by a large elm, its wide low branches ideal shelter. A vibration of emotion stirred behind him. The lad was jittery with anticipation of a barbequed wee beast.

"On you go. Catch your rabbit, lad."

Vygeas barely finished speaking and the lad scurried off into the forest, a small skein of twine in one hand and a sharp stick in the other. The lad had guts. He'd credit that to him. He'd soon see if he had the know-how. Vygeas allowed himself a smile and gathered wood. He scraped a patch of ground clear with his boot and threw down the sticks and dry branches.

A sharp crack of twigs and rustling in the forest came from a different direction than Aiden. Vygeas sniffed.

The human who had followed emitted a scent now blowing on the cool evening air.

Slight nervousness, expectation, and wariness came his way, wafting a mustard tone on the air.

The sounds and the scents came closer. It was a small human. Had Aiden's sister followed? Tension flashed along his neck. *Surely not?* The forest was no place for a small child. Nor was wandering from one's village a safe activity for any female. Especially in the present climate of skirmishes and battles at any turn—not with the calibre of rogue mercenary Lord Ciarán would employ.

Vygeas paused in setting the fire and stood tall. But not he. He was an assassin, it was true, but he held to the honour of his craft.

Mercenaries in Lord Ciarán's warbands suffered no allegiances nor code of conduct. He swallowed hard against the visions rising. If only he could wipe the cries of dying children from his mind.

Vygeas gritted his teeth. He would never return to that life.

He'd rather die.

The crunch of boots on leaf litter came from the forest's edge. He flicked a glance into the trees and grasped the hilt of his dagger. A woman crouched low, trusting the foliage and dimming light to shield her.

Perhaps Lord Ciarán sent her to pursue him. He would not doubt that lord would put hindrances in his way.

Vygeas kept his back to her approach, now busying himself with setting the fire. He should have it blazed down to coals by the time the hunter returned with his kill. Light footsteps left the forest and now treaded right behind him. A faint scent of leather and pine rushed in his direction. A smile teased the corners of his mouth. To underestimate a warrior-woman was to do so at your own peril.

He spun.

"Oh!" The young woman, clad in the leather armour of the south and breeches, skidded to a halt. Dust clouded her boots as she stopped her forward momentum. "I seek travelling companions. You are a warrior. I wish to travel with you. You may be my guard."

Confidence and surety of her request flowed to him across the fire in a wave of strong perfume he could only name as *her*.

"I can pay. Once we reach the destination. You *are* headed to Eilean?" She tilted her head with her query.

Vygeas narrowed his eyes. Her boots were almost new, but the rest of her attire had seen better days, and a travel wariness sat as an aura around her.

"Aye." The scar on his mouth tugged. "But if you are to travel with me, I would know how you handle that weapon." He lifted his chin, indicating the short sword at her belt. "Competence in the martial arts is a requirement in a travelling companion."

The petite woman blinked a querying expression.

"You may join me if you can beat me." He turned his back on her.

Determination chased a heartbeat of hesitation then her emotions hit Vygeas full on the back.

He turned.

Her weapon was on its way up to his torso, the blade blunt. He knocked it aside. She followed through with a would-be-punch from her free hand. He grabbed that wrist with his other hand as he pulled his sword from its scabbard over his shoulder.

Her eyes widened, but frustration flowed from her, colouring the air a soft red. Vygeas brought his broadsword down.

Momentary panic flared from her. His sword locked with her short sword making its way to his face. Hilt to hilt. Body close to body. Her deep-brown eyes opened wider.

It had been a dance. The warrior-woman moved with grace and flexibility but was no match in strength. Her breath was rapid. And sweet. She was a beauty. Long dark curls drawn back with a leather-thong that could not contain the wisps of curl at the side of her oval face. Olive skin. She was from the southern coast, from the clans near the border between Dál Gaedhle and Dál Gallain, if he wasn't mistaken. A noble woman by the look of those cheek bones.

Short swords and hidden blades! What was she doing here, dressed like that, and fighting him?

"Well, aren't you going to say anything?" She was so close her honey breath brushed his face. Her clear diction confirmed his observations. Frustration mixed with annoyance came from her like waves of pointed daggers.

"Who are you?" He was gruff, so he swallowed. He wouldn't add fear into her mix. "Why are you out in the woods alone?" His voice came out softer this time.

"Who are *you*? With that hood you look like a Sage of the Order." White teeth flashed. The front two were crooked.

Vygeas' heart pounded. He'd never met such a woman. She had guts and wits and wasn't afraid to cross him.

"I'm no celibate sage." He stared at her. Her body was still, but her heart tried to fight its way out of her chest.

He released her and nudged her away.

"So, may I?" She flicked her head. "Travel with you?"

"You wish to travel with a man, alone? What are you offering?"

"You're with a knave, aren't you?" She placed her sword-free hand on her hip and pointed to the forest with her blade.

Crashing through the forest's edge, Aiden carried a rabbit.

"My lord, I caught one." Pride echoed in his announcement. He looked from Vygeas to the woman. "My lady." He bobbed his head in a bow. "We'll make it enough for you too."

"Now wait a moment! Who says—?" Vygeas began.

"I'm not a lady!"

"Aye, you are, ma'am. And a warrior-woman from Monsae." Aiden stood straighter.

Vygeas turned to her. She pressed those crooked top teeth onto her lower lip and tilted her head a little.

"Well?" Vygeas cocked an eyebrow.

She shrugged.

"The truth, if you please. If you wish to be our travelling companion." He crossed his arms over his chest and rested the flat of his sword against his collarbone.

Waves of decision traversed her face and her shoulders rose with a deep breath. "I am Leyna and, as I have already indicated, I'm on my way to Eilean. That's in this direction, is it not?" Mild annoyance danced around her words. And something else. A fine sheen of sweat glistened her brow.

"Aye, but I'd like you to answer my young knave's question." Vygeas forced a smile, which usually ended in a tight sneer, but this warrior-lady seemed like the type to handle it. It might allay her anxiety while he wrestled with his own within.

Blades and bows! And double-sided battle-axes! He'd like her to answer Aiden's question.

Monsae. He'd had a contract down there five years ago. Killed a nobleman lord and his lady-wife. Just got out in time to avoid the daughter—a young woman coming home from a ball. She was on the list too. But *nothing* could make him do it.

"How would you know what anyone from Monsae looks like?" She threw her question to Aiden.

"When my Mam and Da died, we went to stay with our cousins but that, well that did nae work out." Aiden's shoulders drooped. "Their village was near the coast."

The lad emitted the scent of grief, which wafted across the fire and hit Vygeas. He held his breath, blocking his nose and stifling the cloying aroma. He would not get too involved.

"Your title, Leyna?" Vygeas released his sword scabbard from around his shoulder and re-sheathed his broadsword.

"Your name first," she challenged, still holding her short sword tight.

"I am Vygeas." He lifted his chin and indicated to his knave. "This is Aiden."

"And title? House?"

"I don't have one." Vygeas clenched his jaw.

"I knew it!" Aiden ducked at the glare Vygeas shot at him.

"In that case, neither do I." Smug satisfaction's perfume made its way from her. "So, may I accompany you? You *are* going to Eilean? This is the only road due south."

Vygeas hesitated. All he'd sensed so far from this woman was honesty. If Lord Ciarán or Drostan had sent her, he'd smell it.

"Aye. To both questions," he answered.

Aiden started a delighted laugh but stifled it as Vygeas turned to him. "You hold my horse!"

"Aye, my lord. No talking."

"And cook that rabbit." His brow tight with a frown, he turned from Aiden who was stoking the fire, and fixed his gaze on the young woman. "What business do you have in Eilean?"

"You first, warrior." She sheathed her sword in its leather scabbard hanging from her belt.

Vygeas tapped his thigh. How much to tell?

"As you see, I am a mercenary on my way to join the combat. But first, I have a task in Eilean."

That will suffice. That the fight would be for his own life, this young noble-woman need not know.

A flash of apprehension emanated from her, its swirl of grey mixed with orange floating by him.

"We will travel west once past Eilean." He did not lie. He would join the Ard Righ's army once free of Lord Ciarán. The High King of Dál Gaedhle, Donnach MacEnoicht, was an honourable ruler. He would add his blade to that man's cause. "The battles rage there. Eilean is yet unaffected by the unrest our land now experiences. But, my lady, your reasons for travelling alone in a climate such as this?" He motioned with his hand for her to begin.

"There's a merchant I wish to make acquaintance." Leyna picked up a large rock with a flat surface and brought it closer to the fire Aiden had brought to life.

The lad does have skills.

"Buying or selling?" Vygeas asked.

Leyna's gaze flicked up to him, confusion hinting in her eyes. She lowered them to the fire. "There's something I wish to give him."

"It must be small, for you carry little."

"It's a letter, actually." Her eyes flicked at the fire. Alarm flowed out from her and buffeted Vygeas with its sharp scent.

She was making up a cover story. What *did* this woman have to hide?

"Fhialain has been unjust to his workers and hasn't paid them for half a year." She blinked indignation. "Their families starve while the man and his family grow fat."

Vygeas pulled up another suitable rock and sat opposite her across from the fire now burning down to coals. Aiden had taken the rabbit off to near the tree line where he'd skinned and gutted it. He poked a sharp green stick through it as he walked back to the fire.

"No' paid his workers! That's cruel." Aiden's sense of the not-fair made itself clear. "I dinnae understand how people get away with it. Why don't the judges in Eilean take him to task?"

Vygeas stared at him, a niggle stirring within. The lad was free with his opinions.

"Your pardon, my lord but I'll not say nothing when people are nae treated rightly." Aiden held the rabbit over the coals and lowered his eyes to it.

"Aye, lad, ye are right to feel the way you do." Vygeas' niggle receded. "Too often the weak are taken advantage of and the judges of this world do nothing. Those who should stand up for those who cannot, do not, and leave the weak and powerless without support. They should be dealt with."

He gave a slight nod at his own justification for the contracts he'd completed.

"When judges and leaders do violence to the Law, someone has to make a stand." Vygeas turned to Leyna. "Well done, my lady. I wish you well with your meeting this merchant." He should warn her to not get too close. When the time came, he'd keep an eye out for her.

The heat from the coals bathed his face as he removed his gloves in preparation for eating. The aroma of roasting rabbit was comforting, soothing his stomach's hurt from lack of food. He had not had reasonable company for some time. Especially not the company of a beautiful woman.

"Why travel alone, Lady Leyna?"

She screwed up her mouth. "I prefer that you didn't call me *lady*, if you please."

"Very well, Leyna, why are you dressed like a brigand?"

"Because she is one." Aiden spoke across the fire. His tone was innocent, and honesty seeped from him. He looked up at the silence. "Pardon, lord. My lady. But I just say what I see." He cringed. "I know. I'm not meant to speak. Just hold the horse. Don't send me home, Nan will never forgive me. I'll take a beating, honest I will—"

"Enough!" Standing up, Vygeas took a halting breath. The boy *had* said enough. As to a beating. "I don't beat young lads, even those who should know better." He sat back on the stone.

"Please, my lord, dinnae send me back. It'll break Nan's heart." Aiden's eyes watered.

"I'll no send ye back. It's all right, calm doon." Vygeas' own commoner accent came out heavily in his words. He blinked at his resolve to not hurt the lad who definitely spoke too much. But Aiden had a point. Vygeas turned to Leyna. Her brown eyes were round, and the knuckles of her clenched hands whitened. It was time for some truth from this woman from Monsae.

"I think if you wish to travel with us, you need to tell us more."

Leyna remained silent for a moment. Her gaze flew from Vygeas to Aiden and back again. The muscles of her slender throat worked.

"Very well. I have lost all. I have nothing else to lose." Her words came out in a tumble along with the delicate scent of release. "As ragged as you two are, you are probably the most honest men I have been with for some time. Think not ill of me for what you are about to hear, but I go to find the man I wish to kill."

"The merchant?" Aiden asked over the almost-cooked rabbit.

"*Weesht*. Let Lady Leyna finish," Vygeas reprimanded.

"No, not the merchant." She looked over the fire to the young lad. At Vygeas' own knave—the honest, open young lad who was wiser than his years but still oblivious to the power of his observations. "The man who will kill the merchant."

Cold now filled Vygeas', leaving no room for his hunger. He forced himself to speak.

"What do you mean, Leyna?"

"Well, the truth is I have been living among a group of thieves." She hesitated, as if deciding what to tell and what not to. "I'm now on my own, but I still hear what goes on. There is a contract on this merchant. A Lord Ciarán has put one out—"

"How do you know of this?" Vygeas could not stop himself from interrupting. "You know Lord Ciarán?"

Her brow creased. "No, I know not this Lord Ciarán, but all are aware of his contract. Well, everyone who moves in those circles, so to speak."

Vygeas raised an eyebrow. Candour flowed from the woman, glowing her a pale blue, and he sensed she truly did not know his employer.

"Continue, if you please," he asked.

"So, every assassin who has heard is after it because they'll be able to take the merchant's riches when they've done the job. Well, the riches that aren't locked away. Anyone with wealth would be foolish not to hide it. But it is said the merchant has riches worth the taking lining his halls."

So, the woman planned to assassinate an assassin. The tension eased from Vygeas' shoulders as, so far, his own true trade remained unknown to her— *And will do so for as long as possible.* Vygeas narrowed his eyes as certain implications hit him like the flat edge of a broadsword.

"And this Lord Ciarán has let it be known? He's not hired anyone specifical-ly?"

"He's made it like a game," she said. "The first to kill the merchant wins not only his wealth, but Lord Ciarán's gold."

Coals popped as the last of the fat dripped from the rabbit. Aiden tore some meat off the cooked wee beast and handed it to Vygeas who held it as he gazed into the fire. Cold, which had tickled his innards, now grabbed them tight.

Competition. He *had* to get to the merchant first and obtain proof he'd killed him, or his own life was over.

Damn that Lord Ciarán. And damn, once again, Drostan who had known it all along.

FIVE

LORD CIARÁN'S TOWER

Drostan leaned over the carved-stone divination bowl, a thoughtful silence filling his workshop in the round tower. His apprentice, Bram, stood quiet and respectful by the solid wooden door and added a *staying* to his, focussing a force on the bolt which held the door closed, and barring Drostan's world from intrusion.

Bram had the angular qualities women swooned over, with dark locks of long wavy hair framing his handsome features, his dark brown, almost black eyes, could pierce a soul. A serious mage, one who would aspire to attain the rank of sorcerer, would soon discover matrimony and family could have no hold on their life. The pledge of a mage to magic surpassed all other allegiances.

Drostan had waited a day before attending to this task assigned to him by his present master. There was prestige attached to this position, the personal mage of a lord, but that meant little to him.

Drostan focused his inner energy and combined it with that of the stone dish. Stone was his medium and his energy source. His skill in accessing it honed from years of study and practice in the magical arts.

It was now, when the power surged through him, that he came alive.

This is why I live. Nothing else compares.

It flowed through his body in waves, rushing through his spirit, bringing meaning to his existence. The energy of the universe...the solid immovable rock in the centre of the whirlwind and flood of this transitory life.

He gasped in the ecstasy he craved, clinging to this magical energy that gave him power over others—such as Vygeas. His lips stretched in a grin, for like Vygeas in the past, if people desired enough, he could make them do *anything*.

The crystal-clear water in the smooth-stone divination bowl became a blue-green background in which a vision emerged, the images' traverse through this conduit strengthening them.

The vision was of a verdant forest.

Leafy.

Cool.

The dawn mist hung low around the trees, the warmth in the day's sunlight yet to chase it away. The energy of the rocks in the ground and the boulders by the road moved through him, sharpening his vision. Leaving his body in the workshop, his soul dived into the bowl and travelled to the vision's location.

Laughter came from the dusty road ahead. One horse, three people walking beside it. A war horse.

Vygeas' war horse.

Drostan moved closer, through the air like a wraith, unseen by the travellers.

Vygeas strode tall, as straight as the trees that flourished at the edge of this road and formed the forest which climbed up the hill beside it. There was a lightness to the warrior-assassin's step not noted at his interview with Lord Ciarán.

An older lad, almost a man, but not, led Vygeas' horse. The stallion lifted his head, eyes widening at Drostan's presence. Drostan sent a *dampening* that covered Vygeas and his stallion. The horse settled back to a calm walk.

A woman strode beside Vygeas.

Interesting. Drostan moved closer. She was a petite woman dressed in leather armour with a short sword belted to her waist. A clear eye, long hair, and well spoken. She was a coastal woman of noble bearing. How did she come into Vygeas' company? And to what purpose?

Oh, Lord Ciarán would relish this information.

"What was that?" The woman shivered.

"What?" Vygeas glanced concern to the woman beside him then looked through Drostan. Drostan pulled back as he sent yet another *dampening* in Vygeas' direction.

"I just felt... oh, nothing." She shook herself.

Drostan retreated.

The clear waters of his stone divination bowl came back into view and with gradual steps he let go of the energy while his spirit returned to his body.

He removed his hands from the bowl's edge and nodded to Bram, who eased his posture as his vigilance reduced. It was fortuitous that this junior mage had come under his tutelage. Similar to himself, Bram had an innate talent for the magic arts and the potential to be a great sorcerer. Just as he had been from his own youth.

Drostan brushed past Bram, strode out of his chambers and down the circular staircase, shedding the last traces of his power. He would never let his lord have a sniff of it.

Reaching Lord Ciarán's private chamber in the tower, he knocked.

"Come." The order was abrupt.

Drostan opened the door of the round tower's small room to a candlelit view of Lord Ciarán's back as he stood in front of a tall bookcase stuffed with books and parchments. A desk, with vellum-bound tomes and scrolls scattered across its wooden surface, sat between them.

"I've just acquired another volume in the series *How the Keltoi Built the World*. Fascinating." Lord Ciarán turned. "What is it?" His comment was as sharp as his aquiline nose.

"I have found him, my lord."

Grey eyebrows rose. "Go on."

"He has companions—"

"Strange." Lord Ciarán stretched the word. "Vygeas usually works alone."

"At present, he has a peasant knave and a noblewoman-warrior with him."

"A lady? Who? Do you recognise her?" Lord Ciarán snapped out his questions.

"No, my lord but she is of coastal stock, brown curly hair, brown eyes, small stature—"

"Yes, yes, I know what coastal people look like. Is she a...?" Lord Ciarán's eyes widened. "No, it's not Lady Leynarve of Monsae, is it?" He paced around the room. "She disappeared when I had her parents disposed of. They never found her body, but that whelp of an assassin said he'd fed her to the dogs." He stopped abruptly, tapping his top teeth with his forefinger, brow creasing in a line above his nose. "I never did achieve all I had wished with that endeavour. Those clansmen warriors loyal to the family were even fiercer in their defence of the caisteal and clan lands once they'd assumed the demise of the whole family. Caused me to retreat."

He snarled and recommenced his pacing. "I vowed to wait for a more opportune time. And now may be it. If this is Lady Leynarve." He stepped to his desk and a scroll caught in his wake rolled off and onto the floor. "Does Vygeas know who she is?"

"I am uncertain that he knows who she may be, my lord. But he was enjoying her company."

"Enjoying her company?" Lord Ciarán shouted. "He's under the presumption that I've given him a chance and he's playing with it. Does he not value his life or is he too stupid to realise it is his last hope?" His shoulders shook and hands trembled. "Although I'd hate to discard a most valuable resource." His face reddened and his mouth contorted as though he struggled to speak. "He is more trouble than he's worth. The assassins I've sent know the real mark and will do their duty, but I *need* her."

Drostan leaned back. He should commence his retreat while he was able.

"Go get the girl. I want her lands and title. An army at her disposal comes with her. I need all the warriors I can muster and with Lady Leynarve as my spouse they cannot refuse."

Drostan didn't move.

"Go on. Why are you standing there?"

"My lord, my power isn't strong outside the caisteal."

Lord Ciarán blinked his lack of comprehension.

"Stone and rock are my conduits, my lord." Drostan bowed as he gave his explanation. "If I leave, I am only strong if I am near them."

"Can't you take a stone with you?" Lord Ciarán's sarcasm hung in the air, then he sighed. "I can't spare the warriors. I'm moving my forces north-east for my campaign. He's one man, you're a wizard, are you not?"

"A mage, sire. I do have powers—"

"Use them. Go! Why can I still see you?"

Drostan left, shut the door behind him, and let out a breath. He needed a plan to get the young woman away from Vygeas. Closer inspection would confirm the woman's identity.

Vygeas...

So, we have encountered one another again in this life?

Vygeas deserved the price of his gifting. *For I* would *have done it.*

Vygeas knew what I was, even then.

Drostan's insides simmered, but he dampened them down.

They had both wounded him deeply and they *both* deserved what they received.

Elyse, her death.

Vygeas, a lifetime of torment.

He huffed and, nostrils flaring, dragged his source from the caisteal walls to temper his soul's renewed pain.

Calm ensued and he ran up the circular stair to his room and opened the door. Bram stood by the shelves, where he kept his apothecary stores and replaced the lid on a clay pot of dried elder flower.

"The old methods are always the best." Drostan rubbed his hands together. "Divide and conquer."

"My master?" Bram's brow crinkled, making no dint in his handsome features.

"Mayhap I can distract the assassin enough to miss his mark—lose his freedom and his life." Drostan's face tightened, stretching the corners of his mouth. "I go on a journey, my young apprentice. You must hold vigil until my return." He grabbed a leather satchel. "I will have to stay close to my conduit, but the way to Eilean is strewn with standing stones."

Drostan allowed a momentary snarl, then released it and faced Bram. "The peoples of the area's past worshipped with henges. And, like those who also worshipped trees and fire and such elements, they knew nothing of the true power they contain." He waved his hand dismissively as he gathered his supplies.

Bram's eyes lit with understanding.

"Nor did they comprehend how to wield it." Drostan continued the impromptu lesson. "Or the true sources of power in this world. I head for the nearest standing stone, Bram. With a fast enough horse, I shall get there before the warrior and his company."

He rummaged through a pile of stones sitting in a wide-necked clay pot, each one the size of a man's hand.

"The warrior owes me all. When I was younger, before I gained access to study on the learned isle, I practiced my magic from a cave just outside of the village where that warrior grew up. All said I could grant each their heart's desire." Drostan leaned toward Bram, dropping his voice in a conspiratorial manner. "And that I could, for I had learned much. I...had already met my true master." He straightened then. "Of more you shall learn in time."

"Ye know him? The prisoner recently released?"

"Aye. Vygeas. Lord Ciarán's assassin. He came from peasant stock but wished to be a warrior and sought magical gifting to that end. As you well know, magic comes at a cost. I enticed Vygeas, worked on his insecurities, offered a magic gift of heightened senses as well as exceptional prowess in the martial arts. He gave all to have the skills he wished." Drostan narrowed his eyes. "A warrior can do much with the anger arising from a broken heart. It fuels the motives, drives the darkest instincts, keeps the edge on hate. And hate leaves a fighter not content without a kill."

"Why do *you* hate this Vygeas so?" The words flew from Bram. "If you pardon my boldness, my master."

"Vygeas took my only chance at love."— *Oh, how that burns to say it*— "But love means naught to me now."

"Then why your hatred still, my master? When as a mage dedicated to magic...love is not for us?"

Searing heat crept up Drostan's face. "Because he did."

Six

The Road to Eilean

Warmth from the silver sun seeped into Leyna's shoulders while the mountains surrounding her transitioned to soft rounded hills still retaining their purple coating. The heather in bloom cast its magic mauve hue on either side as she marched along with Vygeas. Copses of ash and alder grew close beside the road, and ahead the terrain flattened to broad expanses of green lowlands patched with the deeper green hues of forests and the sandy brown where boulders clumped together. Stone henges were commonplace in these parts and far off in the distance a circle of stones caught her view. There would be many along their path to Eilean. She wasn't one for following the gods, but she always regarded these sacred places with respect.

She took a deep breath, inhaling the pure air blowing from the southern sea. A faint salt-tinge lingered, like the air of her long-lost home. That empty place inside, in the shape of her parents, stirred with its tang. She would soon fill this void with the satisfaction of seeing their assassin dead. Her mouth tightened, but she forced herself to relax. She must not draw attention.

Tall Vygeas strode beside her, setting quite a pace. If he rode his stallion, he'd leave them far behind. The fact of assassins gathering on Eilean urged her to hasten their journey, but Vygeas, herself, and Aiden would not fit on that horse together. He frowned, facing the road ahead, slowing his pace slightly, giving her time to catch up with his longer strides. Vygeas was a considerate travelling companion despite his own seemingly pressing need to get to Eilean. He was rough but a gentleman beneath the scars and leather armour.

Definitely not a nobleman.

"Where did you learn to fight?" she asked.

Vygeas' jerked around to face her. His teeth caught his scarred lip.

"I don't mean to pry. It's just that you're so good. You anticipate like no other warrior I've fought. It was as if you knew exactly what I would do before I did. I don't imagine the warrior sages trained you. Not being of noble birth." Leyna trailed off as Vygeas' expression hardened.

He closed his mouth tight, lips thinning and the scar on the right-hand corner of his mouth puckering with the pressure. "A sage trained me at first but, as you know, it's frowned upon for a warrior sage to instruct a commoner, so I learned through experience." Vygeas' eyes narrowed as his gaze pinned her. "Not all learn from a sage. Some who do can become overconfident. Such as thinking a blunt blade will give success in combat against an opponent twice their size."

Leyna faced the road ahead, determined to not respond to his goading. So, Vygeas didn't wish to say more about himself. But how could he learn such anticipation of an opponent's moves? Experience without training got you killed.

"Who is your lord?" she asked.

"My employ is with no one lord." The humour from their morning's conversations had well and truly gone from his voice.

Birdsong floated from the trees and a buck honked in the distance while their own footsteps and the war horse's hooves continued their march.

"What can a warrior sage teach me that I cannot teach myself?" Vygeas spoke with ill-restrained vehemence. "I wasn't good enough for them, but they're not the only way to receive instruction in the martial arts."

"Your pardon, sir. I meant no disrespect." Leyna rubbed her chin, her cheeks heating.

Vygeas breathed through his nose, the noise loud in her ear. "All I wanted was to be more than a farmer's son, but the nobility, and even my faither, forbade it."

Leyna spun to look at him speaking his honest words. Until now, he had been gruff, but it seemed her question had sparked a memory of struggle in his own history—a contention with the status quo.

"Well, that wasn't enough for me." Vygeas' hands gestured in sharp motions, as if wielding a pretend sword. "So, I did what I could, and made myself a warrior." He straightened, his chest puffing at his achievement.

Leyna smiled up at him, her shoulders relaxing at his determination. She'd done the same—turned her back on convention.

Perhaps Vygeas was a kindred spirit.

"So, answer the question, my lady." His features softened. "What is it I can only learn from a sage?" His hazel gaze rested on her, long lashes shadowing his cheeks.

A flutter hinted inside her.

Focus!

Leyna lightened her step. Vygeas blinked and fell into step with her once more.

"You could learn that the enemy isn't always the one you see."

Vygeas cocked an eyebrow.

"There is an enemy within you," she explained. "Hindering you. Everyone has one. You must face it. Sometimes it stops you dead and you can't go on until you deal with it. You must discover what is yours, sell-sword."

Vygeas' eyebrow remained cocked, and his step missed a beat. He soon did a double-take and caught up with her. Either he'd never heard such things before, or her words touched something inside him.

Leyna chastised herself. Who was she to speak this way to anyone? Not a sage, that was for certain. *Or is it my own inner demons demanding attention?*

"My lord?" Aiden had been silent for some time.

"Aye?" Vygeas stepped up to the lad. Leyna moved close also, as the lad spoke with concern.

"How far is it to Eilean, my lord?"

"We would need to walk all day to make it in three." Leyna allowed no time for Vygeas to answer.

Vygeas grimaced. He'd set a hard pace. "I have heard the merchant plans to sail for more wares."

"Well, he could do so soon," Leyna replied. "The trade winds blow consistent this time of year and he would wish to return before the winter storms when vessels anchor in safe harbour."

"You know these lands, my lady." Vygeas faced her, holding a pensive expression. "Monsae lands are not far from here. So, what do you suggest?"

Ahead in the direction of the coast, dark clouds gathered. The weather was turning. The wind could whip the rain and mist in off the sea and be upon them with no notice.

"There is a bothy almost half a day's walk from here. If we speed our pace, we could reach it by nightfall and sleep there. The weather's coming in and it will probably rain by then."

"Very well," Vygeas nodded. "That we shall do."

Warmth settled in her and she let only the corner of her mouth take up the smile. Acceptance was a kind thing and Vygeas had given it willingly.

"Pardon me, my lady, but what is a bothy?" Aiden asked.

"You seem so worldly wise and yet you know not what a bothy is?" Leyna raised both her brows but gave a reassuring smile. This young man was talkative and very likable.

Aiden shook his head.

"It's a traveller's code." Vygeas took the reins from Aiden.

Dräger snorted. The horse hung his head and nibbled at his bit, bored from walking at a human's pace all day.

"Aye. We can stay, cook over its hearth and sleep on the floor under its shelter in relative safety. We must be respectful to whoever else stays there." Leyna placed her hand on the tall lad's arm.

"What if brigands are staying there?" Aiden's arm tensed beneath her hand.

She pressed her lips together for his concern was warranted.

"Then we move on." Vygeas' voice reached her from the other side of Dräger.

"And sleep in the rain anyway." The lad slumped his walk, his feet shuffling.

"We take our chances." She rubbed his back. The road had been quiet so far, maybe they would have the bothy to themselves.

Despite Leyna's shoes being worn-in by their previous owner, her feet burned from their rubbing by the time the bothy came into view. The sky ahead darkened with both the gathering night and rain clouds.

The bothy was a rectangular stone structure with a chimney at both ends and a recently re-thatched roof. Someone had oversight of it and, inside, a swept stone floor revealed their care. One fireplace was large and more than adequate for warmth with plenty of room for cooking. Twigs and logs sat ready in the grate. Straw mats lay stacked against the back wall.

"Ooh. We'll have a comfy bed tonight." Leyna cast her gaze around the room.

"This is the best one I've ever seen." Vygeas nodded his approval.

"Where's the—?" Aiden's face pinked. "Where do we—?"

"Outside," Leyna and Vygeas spoke in unison.

"But there's not a—"

"Trees," Vygeas answered. "Take that spade and dig a hole first." He pointed with his chin to the implement by the door and the lad ran out.

"I'll light the fire." Leyna got her flint out of her bag. "We have nothing to cook, but we'll need light and heat. The rain will cool things down. I can feel it in the air already." She squatted before the dry tinder and wood of the pre-set fire.

Vygeas chose the best of the straw mats and placed them in a row by the fire. "I've some dry meat and a chunk of cheese. It's a little old but we can share."

"I have a handful of biscuits." The spark hit the bark Leyna teased, and it smouldered. She encouraged it to life with a breath and nurtured it further with twigs.

"So, the lady can live it rough." Vygeas leaned his shoulder against the stone fireplace, watching her.

A strand of his hair came loose from its tie, catching on his two-day growth as it fell across his face. His strong jaw caught the light from the now blazing fire and his hazel eyes held a fire of their own. Leyna swallowed, drowning out the thump of her racing heart. His large hands rested on his dagger's hilt. His stance was relaxed, and his attention focused on her. Heat rose to her face, and not from the fire.

Vygeas was an unusual man. Quiet, yet full of passion which erupted from him when prodded, as it had that afternoon. Leyna warmed inside at his fervour—it was like her own. And at present, they both had intentions to kill. A shiver passed through her.

Vygeas squatted onto his haunches beside her and raised his palms to the fire. He was uncultured, but he was kind. A sell-sword paid for his skills...But isn't that what she'd done for the last five years? Thieves of elegant and costly items were of a similar ilk—but without the violence...on most occasions. She'd been paid in kind for her particular talent.

But no, Vygeas was more than just a sell-sword. He had exceptional skills. He was continually observing his environment. She'd watched him as they journeyed. Vygeas had often noticed something long before she had.

"What have you done apart from fight in the armies of other men?" Leyna dragged her gaze off his jaw.

Vygeas straightened and stood, blinking away the expression his eyes held. His Adam's apple bobbed as the fire crackled, but he did not answer.

Leyna bit her lip. "What I mean is, do you know any assassins? You see, I go to find the one who murdered my parents, but I know not for whom I seek."

Vygeas' cheek hardened. "Aye, I have encountered some in my travels." His words were tight.

"Have you heard of any completing...their task...in Monsae?"

Vygeas blinked but remained silent. His throat worked again.

The door burst open.

"There's something out there," Aiden shouted. The lad was pale, and his hands trembled.

The echo of Dräger's nervous nickering came through the open door. Vygeas' sword sung as he drew it from its sheath. "Stay here. I'll check."

"But I can—" She stepped forward, grasping the handle of her short sword.

"Stay here." Vygeas' voice was firm.

"I'll not remain here." Her indignation laced her tone. "I'll come with you."

Vygeas placed his hand in the centre of her chest. It was wide and warmed where it contacted.

"No need endangering two of us. Stay with the boy." His brows knit together above his hazel gaze, stopping her mid-stride.

Vygeas stepped out into the rainy night, shutting the door behind him.

SEVEN

THE BOTHY

Drostan peered from behind the boulder. Vygeas had searched and found nothing, settled his stallion, and returned to the bothy. Drostan rested his chin on the rock, its firm cool seeping into his jaw and transferring through his robe to his flesh. The stone structure of the bothy was ideal.

How fortuitous. He couldn't have chosen better himself.

He turned and leaned with his back to the boulder. It was an adequate conduit, and the stone-built bothy offered excellent amplification. Blocking Vygeas' acute senses and making him blind to his presence had been simple magic.

He had ridden hard to catch up with his targets and his limbs were heavy with fatigue, but he did not require physical strength for this task.

I give thanks to you my spirit lord, Cumhachd adhar. Power of the air

He turned and faced the bothy. The flickering of light, indicating movement within, ceased. The weary travellers settling down for the night, no doubt. Drostan relaxed, drew a breath and his source with it, then moved his soul out of his body, up and over the boulder and through the walls of the bothy, as silent as the night through which he floated.

The travellers lay side by side on the sleeping mats, the lad nearest the fire. Drostan laughed silently. He had given the youth a good scare. Sown the mood. He hovered over the curly-head and twirled a wisp of thought and let it gently descend.

He moved on and hovered over the adults. Vygeas and Lady Leynarve lay close. The assassin and noblewoman's barriers were eroding. That would not last. Drostan need not suggest, merely draw memories to the surface of these two dreamers. Both had fears. Co-operative demons to awaken and work for him throughout the night. Drostan slipped out and away back to his body draped behind the stone, where he lingered and relished the surge of power, holding on to every tendril his spirit could grasp until forced to relinquish it.

Aiden lays on his side, hugging his knees to his chest. The floor touches cold to his hip and shoulder. Welts on his back and buttocks burn where the twitch had snapped his skin apart with each stroke, overriding the floor's chill.

What wrong have I done? Why does Uncle treat me so?

Mam had said 'Always be honest', and that truthfulness was an honourable trait in a man. Aiden would please her and be the man she wished him to be.

Mam may not be here anymore, but I will keep her close—no matter how hard they beat me.

Light shines in the upper tower. Leyna's parents must be waiting up for her. She laughs and steps lightly up the stone staircase, the soft swish of her dress proclaims its expensive material. The same rustle had accompanied each dance with every young man at the ball. Sons of lords and noblemen-warriors alike had chosen her for a turn around the floor.

She pushes her loose curls behind her ear and knocks on the solid wood of her parents' chamber door.

"Mama? Papa? You waited up for me?"

Quiet answers her. It is past the first watch of the night, and they must have dozed off. Leyna turns the lever with gentle hands. The door opens to a moonlit room, a draft chills her face. The light curtains at the balcony moving in the breeze catches her eye. A boot and the edge of a long grey coat flash out of sight and over the balcony wall.

Silent bodies lay in her parents' bed. A candle flickers, strobing the gaping throats and the river of blood flowing from their bed.

Leyna steps closer, cold now encompasses her whole body. She reaches out and scoops Papa into her shaking arms, his cooling warmth presses against her. She lays his head back on his pillow and runs to the other side of the bed. Her feet scoot out from beneath her and she falls onto Mama's gurgling neck. She jumps on the bed between them, holding them both close, one with each arm. She wills them back, as their blood paints her dress their life's colour.

"I want to be a great warrior." Vygeas stands in front of the young mage who leans over a small pool in a rocky ledge far back in the cave. The hot spring, which pours from the mountain just outside the village, runs through it. Droplets of the thermal water drip from the roof of the grotto while more trickles through the dark slime that coats its walls.

He had heard this novice mage could grant you your heart's desire.

"It'll cost." Drostan's face reflects the images displayed in the shallow stone pool before him—his makeshift divination bowl.

"I have no coin. You know that. I've spent it all on weapons and coaching."

"What would you do to be the best?"

"Anything." Vygeas' desperation is clear in his plea, but he's beyond embarrassment.

"Anything?" Drostan leans forward. "Do this, and I will give you the advantage. Your sight and hearing will be exceptional, no scent will escape you. You will taste their fear, smell their emotions, discern their intentions, see the way before they have thought of it. Do you like the sound of that?"

Vygeas pulse races, reverberating in his ears. That edge is what he requires. With it he will better any warrior—noble or common.

"Aye." Determination pushes caution aside. "What must I do?"

"Kill her." Drostan points to his bowl.

Vygeas deciphers the image reflected on Drostan's face.

It is Elyse.

"No." The thudding of his pulse doubles as he loses control of his breathing.

"How much do you want it?" Drostan's accusing tone echoes in the small cave that now suffocates Vygeas.

"I'll no' kill my love."

Is this man mad?

"But I've *seen* her." Evil permeates Drostan's every word. "Now I *know* her."

"What are ye saying?" Vygeas' pulse kicks up another notch.

"Kill her. Receive your gift. Or I will torture Eylse for all eternity." Drostan's face contorts in a greedy sneer. "It is a truth ye can be certain of, Vygeas Innësson. Either way, I *have* her."

"What!" Vygeas covers his mouth with a shaking hand. The mage has given others their wish for the wise old women in the village tell of his doings and vouch for the certainty of his claims.

Vygeas' guts lurch. Bile bathes his tongue in acid's burn. Elyse now in Drostan's sight, now in danger, for with the power this mage already has he *can* do as he threatens...torment Elyse for all time in a dark empty place beyond this life.

His vision blurs.

He sits under a tree. The dappled sunlight glistens on Elyse's golden hair that nestles around her face and falls to her shoulders in glowing blonde locks. Her weight rests in his lap. His sword hand lies around her throat. He drops his grip. His finger marks remain as indentations on her neck. Elyse's lips are blue and her eyes stare into his, trickling tears.

Vygeas shudders.

"Farewell, my love." His sobs shake him and a pink hue surrounds Elyse's cooling body. He breathes deep, steadying the shaking that reaches his soul, and speaks once more. "Be in the place of peaceful rest. This is all I can give you now."

He had done it. Such unfair choice. What diabolical compulsion. Now *he* lives in hell.

Grass rustles as a vole walks blindly beneath the ash tree on the other side of the copse. A capercaillie high on the mountain above calls to his mate, rattling Vygeas' eardrums. The rich aroma of love and trust surrounds him, mixing with question and disbelief. He buries his face in her hair...

Vygeas awoke screaming.

His heart pounded, thunking right to his temples. He breathed it away. The dream. So real. Perhaps a vision. He grabbed his forehead, clenching hair tight. *Elyse!*

She would be there. In that paradise he hoped for. Safe from the mage's torments. He had ensured it. And lived with the guilt every day since.

Every. Day. Since.

Eight

The Aftermath

Screams other than Vygeas own met his ears, the remnants of his night-terror subsiding, leaving a dull ache in his soul, as empty as his arms which once held Elyse.

Beside him, Leyna lay weeping, her hands covering her face and soft cries muffling into her palms. Her shoulders trembled and her body heaved.

"Leyna?" Vygeas placed his hand on her arm, hitting him with a deep sorrowful grief.

Leyna flinched, moving away from his tentative touch. He tightened his lips, acknowledging his own hurt at her rejection. Vygeas exhaled, blowing away the emotions that had suddenly filled the small bothy and shouted at his heightened senses.

Suffocating. Deafening. Blinding.

Soft sobbing came from beside the fire.

"Oh, Mam." Aiden spoke his words through sleep.

Aiden shivered as if in snow, despite his proximity to the fireplace. The fire had burned to coals and spilled a red hue over the lad.

"I'm sorry. But Mam wanted...I will nae do it again, I promise. Don't..." Aiden's shoulders trembled violently, and his legs thrashed about, shaking Leyna out of her tears. She sat up and scooted closer to the youngster and made soothing sounds while she rubbed his back.

Vygeas stood and joined her, squatting over the boy, grateful for the diversion from his own dream-memory. He would leave his night's vision far behind him as the young lad remained in his.

"Wake him up." Vygeas placed his hand on the lad's shoulder and pressed.

"Oh!" Aiden sat up in his bedding, his wide eyes staring into Vygeas' face.

"All is well." Leyna's voice shook, then she swallowed. "Aiden, it is all a dream." Her voice cleared. "We are here. Whatever you are dreaming, it's not happening."

"But it did," Aiden sobbed. "It wasn't a night-terror. It was real. A memory, my lady. Not my imaginings." His damp cheeks gleamed reddish in the fire's lambent light.

Leyna breathed in sharply and made to speak, but then hesitated. "It was the same for me," she finally said. "Aye." Her voice was just above a whisper. "Something I will never forget but wish to never remember." She wiped the glistening wet away from her cheeks with the heel of her hand.

Vygeas took his blanket from his bedroll and placed it over Aiden's still shaking shoulders. A deep hurt came from the boy but, oddly, no sense of resentment.

"They beat me." Aiden's voice held a pain that wrenched at Vygeas' insides. The lad sent his blue stare his way.

"I promise you. No one will beat you again." Vygeas stood and the lad's shoulders ceased their trembling. Aiden allowed Leyna to place her arm around him.

"It helps to share your troubles, my mam always said." Aiden sniffed. "If ye dinnae mind me sayin' so." He turned to Leyna. "My lady, you are distressed as well. Tell us your dream, if you please."

Leyna's soothing strokes on Aiden's back stopped. She dropped her hand and with it clasped the other resting in her lap.

"It was when my parents were murdered. I will not speak of it. Will not recount it...it is too awful." Leyna stood, grief floating around her as a grey, grey aura. She stepped to the fire and threw on wood, stoking it back to life. The room lit with its strengthening flame while she stood with her back to him.

Vygeas closed his eyes, giving in to her grief, desolation, and anger that filled the room and surrounded him. No, not only surrounded him, but penetrated his soul. To the place where the remnants of his conscience resided.

How many times had he murdered?

Assassinated?

Aye, he'd only taken marks who caused the death of others and whose removal from the lives of those they'd maltreated would bring release to the oppressed and wronged. That was his restriction in his life as an assassin—only those worthy of it had received death by his blade. Except for that time Lord Ciarán had lied—

"My lord?" Aiden pulled him back to the present. "Did you dream?"

"No, lad."

"Aye, you did." Leyna spun from the fire. "Your scream woke me!"

Deep brown eyes bore into his and her accusation flew across the room toward him like a dart.

"Aye, then. I did." Vygeas hung his head.

"Then, you will share—?"

"Nae, I will *not* share." Vygeas pivoted on his heel, grabbed his coat and sword, and threw open the door.

Dragon's blaze!

What would I say? In truth he was a weapon for hire, but if Leyna should find out he'd killed the only woman he'd ever truly loved just to get the advantage...An ache beyond consoling rose to the surface for a moment and caught his breath, then retreated as he pushed down hard once more. Stamping on it.

"Where are you going?" Leyna spoke, stepping toward him.

"I'll saddle Dräger." His voice was gruff. "You pack up. We need to remove ourselves from this place." The door banged behind him— an impotent block to the waves of perceived rejection emanating from his companions and beating at his back.

The slam of the bothy door came to Drostan's ears. He opened his eyes to the last of the night, the horizon now a dim glow as the sun prepared for this coming day's journey across the sky. Sleep's heaviness weighted his limbs.

He must be more attentive!

Near the bothy, Vygeas' war horse nickered softly. Drostan peered around his boulder. Vygeas threw the saddle over his stallion and jerked the girth strap tight. The muscles in his cheeks tightening with a clench as his horse chewed on the bit, flicking his head, and whipping his wet mane in Vygeas' face. Vygeas' vision sat mid-distance. The man distracted by the night's visions, no doubt.

Drostan drew from rock and shielded himself from Vygeas' perception.

The door opened and Lady Leynarve of Monsae walked toward the assassin. Lady Leynarve's memories should now spark some recognition of the man with whom she chose to travel. She handed equipment to Vygeas. Her eyes were red-rimmed, and no smile lit her face as it had on his earlier observations of their journey.

Good, Lady Leynarve was sending him off. As per Drostan's own plan, they would now separate, divided by their dreams. The boy followed them out, hunched over and dishevelled. The rain had started again, and the once-companions looked as *driech* as the weather. Vygeas loaded his stallion and walked away.

No goodbyes. No fond farewells.

Success!

Drostan relished the lightness in his spirit and fixed his gaze on Vygeas' retreating form as his war horse's hoof beats receded along the road.

Lady Leynarve placed her hand on the arm of the knave, and they both walked away from the bothy. So, she would have the young whelp to guard her. The lady would be an easy snatch. A sense of victory arose within him, and he stepped from behind his rock.

A horse whinnied ahead, an uncomfortable animal call.

"Are ye coming!" Vygeas' shouted words travelled back to the pair by the bothy. "We must hasten to Eilean. No more dawdling!"

The boy and the lady-warrior picked up their pace and were soon out of sight.

What? Drostan snuck back to his sarsen-rock.

Impossible!

He let out a harsh huff. Had they not argued? Had Lady Leynarve not called Vygeas out? Demanded he reveal his true self?

Damnation!

And his lord expected a report each day. Maybe he could forestall it.

The success of *that* plan depended on the disposition of Lord Ciarán this day.

Gritting his teeth, he reached into his robe and withdrew a shallow bowl carved from a smooth, white beach pebble, which fitted into his open palm. He stepped to the nearest puddle where the patter of soft raindrops caused miniature rings, distorting the grey sky reflected off its surface. He dipped his bowl in, filling it with the morning's precipitation.

Leaning back against the boulder that had shielded him during the night, he stilled himself and fixed his intentions on his divination cup. His faithful apprentice should be at his post.

A face shimmered in the water—long and angular with a strong jawline and hair as black as night.

"Master?"

Drostan centred himself and focused. "Aye, Bram."

"Lord Ciarán is enquiring of your progress, master." The dark eyes darted away, then returned to him. "He wishes to know if you have...my Lord Ciarán, sir, he cannot hear you."

"Tell me, my apprentice. Are you alone?"

"No, master. Lord Ciarán insisted I look for you in the divination bowl."

Heat burned in Drostan. "Tell him to remove himself from my chambers!" He threw his words at the portable divination bowl in his hand.

"My master, he is Lord Ciarán, your benefactor. I cannot order him." The image of his apprentice shimmered. "Lord Ciarán says," Bram turned his face away and spoke. "I dare not say that my lord—"

"Tell me!" Drostan narrowed his eyes.

In the reflective vision, the young man straightened, and his features hardened as his face turned back to the divination bowl in Drostan's chambers. "My master, your lord wishes me to say that you will return with the Lady Leynarve, or you will have no benefactor, no post, no prospects." The young man's Adam's apple bobbed, then he flinched and the ripples in the pebble-divination bowl obliterated Drostan's view.

Drostan's nostrils flared. The impudence of that lord! He could fare very well without the arrogant nobleman-lord who was full of his own self-importance. The man was a convenience at present and a means to settling an old score.

Vygeas.

Drostan spoke a precautionary incantation that would continue to cloak himself from Vygeas, then marched to where he had tethered his horse the previous night. He would follow closely, seeking the opportunity for a well-rehearsed skill. Changing one's form, as some mages do, was beneath him. He preferred to control the animal for his purposes, not become one himself, even if it was only momentarily. He had practiced the enchantment alongside Bram. Bram had shown promise. Drostan snorted. Aye, the junior mage had great potential.

He reached his gelding, placed the bridle over its head, and re-saddled it. He screwed his mouth in thought for he had rarely tried manipulation on a large animal and when accomplished it had taken its toll on his energy. It was necessary to be in total contact with stone for the process to be successful. He mounted and galloped to the road lined with forest, along which Vygeas and his companions had headed.

"Within that forest, I will seek my rock conduit and a suitable beast."

NINE

THE JOURNEY CONTINUES

Vygeas led Dräger and kept quiet. He would not speak of his dream. He shook his head slowly. It had been a weird night. First, he'd let the firelight make him lose his senses with the woman, and then he'd screamed his way out of a nightmare!

He trudged throughout the morning and into the late afternoon. Dense forests of pine lined either side of the sodden road. Leyna stepped wordlessly beside him, and Aiden plodded staring at the ground. A thick dark cloud wept rain on the distant mountains. He traipsed, his cloak soggy, with Leyna and Aiden just as soaked, splashing through brimming puddles that were like miniature lochs. Droplets gathered on Dräger's mane, matching those running down Vygeas' hair and sticking stray strands to his face. The scent of wet horse surrounded him.

His companions' aromas eased as the day progressed. The rejection he had sensed from them at the bothy had lessened and they seemed more absorbed with their own inner hurts.

Vygeas dare not ask. It would all be bad. Hurt and grief— no doubt stirred up by their dreams— had reduced to a trickle throughout this day's journey. But was still there.

What was in that bothy? An evil spirit. A *deamhan* sent to stir up strife?

A stag honked nearby. It was mating season and it would be a male deer keeping his does in line and warning other males to stay away. Vygeas sensed aggression as it flowed to him in waves from the forest, joining with the assault on his nose of a musky stale urine stink—the distinct scent of a male deer. The bark-like honk sounded once more, this time much louder and closer.

"Look at the magnificent creature." Leyna pointed to a russet stag emerging from the trees to their right.

A full set of antlers crowned the mature male's skull, fourteen tines. All had lost their velvety covering and were hard as bone. The stag raised his head, sniffing the air and then stared directly at Vygeas.

"Ah, my lord?" Caution shimmered orange from Aiden.

The stag stomped and barked, its full attention on them.

"Aye, keep walking."

Dräger gave a screechy nicker, acknowledging the stag's warning. Vygeas continued a few paces along the roadway and the stag stepped further out from the tree line.

"All will be well if we do not cross the path between the stag and his harem," Leyna advised.

"I see no does, my lady." Aiden kept his stare on the stag.

The male deer raised his majestic head, lowered the tines over his back, let out a loud honk, and stomped heavily on the ground before them. The stag's eyes never left Vygeas.

"Get on Dräger." Vygeas' command was sharp as he grabbed Leyna under her arms and lifted her into the saddle. "Ye can ride, my lady?" he threw the reins to her.

"Of course," Leyna said as he boosted Aiden into the saddle behind her. "What of yourself, sell-sword?" Her question hung in the air.

Vygeas slapped Dräger's rump and with an alarmed neigh, the horse cantered away.

"Vygeas!" Leyna's cry trailed behind them.

The stag showed no interest in the war horse and charged toward Vygeas. Head lowered and antlers foremost, the massive animal fixed its intent on Vygeas. Muscles rippled under thick russet-brown fur.

Charger's breath! It was as if he faced a fully armed war horse. Those tines looked sharp.

Vygeas drew his broadsword. Fractions of time were all he needed, and all he had. But it would not be like fighting a man. What would this animal do? He had no sense of anticipation. As if it were erased. He must fight relying on his wits and skill alone.

With the beast almost upon him, Vygeas stepped aside, letting it thunder by. Sharp points missed his side by a dagger blade's width. Vygeas spun, his hair flying in the breeze stirred by the beast's wake. The animal skidded to a halt, lowered its head and, with natural weapons forward, turned on Vygeas once more. He stepped aside, but the stag kept him in his line of charge. Gripping his broadsword's handle tight in both hands, Vygeas braced himself for impact, shoulders tight and upper arms firm.

The stag came level and he crossed both branches of antlers with one stroke. The beast flicked his head, wrenching his broadsword from his grip and sent the blade flying.

The beast travelled on, carried by its own momentum. Vygeas ran behind it and retrieved his weapon. He spun. He now stood in the centre of the road, and the roaring animal charged once more. Sweat dripped from Vygeas and cool prickled at his neck.

It had been such a while since he felt as now.

No impression of this opponent's intentions. No advantage. No—

The beast tore toward him like a boulder careening down a mountain, tines directed at *him*. An array of knives determined to stab him. Vygeas stepped left, then right, as if to dodge the oncoming points. The animal equally countered each move he made and was now rapid in its approach.

Upon him in seconds, they locked weapons. Vygeas' broadsword hooked between the outer tines of each antler. He held his sword's handle and its blade at the flat edge, his gloved hands either side of the chandelier of spikes. Holding his arms straight kept the beast at bay and the daggers of nature from tearing at his flesh.

He danced with the beast in a circle, as if at a local cèilidh. The only music playing was animal grunts and his own cries. Vygeas' boots slid in the moist dirt of the road. The animal skidded him back and forth as he strained to keep his arms straight, ensuring the antler tines were at length. Losing this position would mean a killer blow if the stag sliced his exposed under arm. He would bleed to his death.

Thunk, thunk.

The stag flinched. Two dagger handles stuck out from the animal's right side. One in its thick neck and the other high in its shoulder. Yet another *thud*, and a knife skidded off the back of the gyrating animal. The stag flung back its head, disconnecting Vygeas and his sword from its antlers.

Arms burning from exertion, Vygeas dived out of the way of the now flailing stag. It honked and twisted as if to dislodge the blades embedded in its neck and shoulder. Now lying in the mud, Vygeas rolled, avoiding hooves whooshing air past his head and then his back. He scrambled up and away from the road as the stag galloped off, roaring its pain.

Vygeas leaned back against the trunk of an ancient tree, following the course of the staggering deer, chest heaving. He re-sheathed his broadsword with shaking hands. The encounter had been a matter of moments but the after-effects of a fight, whether with man or beast, always lasted longer. Vygeas blinked. A throwing knife sat in the mud; its edge shiny sharp. He took a pace toward it.

"Vygeas!" Leyna's shout reached him as he slipped the knife from the mud. She came on foot from the forest's edge. "Are you hurt?"

"Nae." He frowned, still panting. "Where are Aiden and Dräger?"

"Aiden is coming." Leyna pointed along the way they had taken.

Dräger cantered toward them with Aiden sitting loosely in the saddle. The lad approached, his expression a mixture of concentration and fear, purple flying off him like sparks from the fire.

Vygeas could sense it! The lad's emotions were now clear to him. His gift had returned. He breathed out heavily as concern's warmth hit him in the face.

"You are uninjured?" Disbelief mingled with relief, swirled from Leyna, and wrapped itself around him.

"I am well, Leyna." Vygeas straightened and held out the knife. "Is this yours, my lady?"

"Aye." Her answer was soft, and she grabbed the throwing knife from his hands.

"So, you are skilled in more than thievery."

Leyna stared at her knife, lips tight, then wiped the soiled blade on a patch of grass and tucked it into her boot. Aiden reached them and pulled Dräger to a stop.

"My lord? You are whole?" Aiden's rumpled brow reached his curly forelock. "You survived the mad stag!" He jumped from the stallion.

"Aye, I have come from my encounter with the beast unscathed. I believe I must direct my gratitude to Leyna." Vygeas bowed to her. "My thanks to you, my Lady Leyna."

Dagger's whisper, but she could handle a knife!

Leyna's cheeks flushed red. "Well, that is why we are travelling companions. Safety in the many."

"Remind me to never turn my back to you when your temper is up." He cocked a half smile.

"My lady, you killed the stag?" Aiden's eyes widened, his gaze on Leyna as if appraising her for the first time. Awe emanated from the lad.

"I did not kill the beast. Only startled it. It ran off." Leyna tilted her head, straightened her leather chest armour, and fiddled with the ties. "It has truly gone?" She looked down the road.

Vygeas turned and scanned as far as he could see and sensed the only beings around were of good intent.

"Aye." He cleared his throat and wiped the raindrops from his brow with his gloved hand.

The drizzle, which had persisted, was now heavy rain.

"We must seek shelter." Leyna stood tall with authority in her tone.

"We cannot afford any holdup." Vygeas covered his head with the hood of his coat.

"We are all wet. Becoming ill with the ague will cause more of a delay." Leyna raised her eyebrows at him. "We will find shelter and light a fire so we all can dry out before proceeding."

Vygeas pressed his lips together and faced her.

Leyna placed her hand on her hip. "Think of the lad. Would you return him to his family unwell?"

No, I would leave him with a healer and proceed without him.

But Leyna would not wish to hear such a retort. The lad's hair hung as rats' tails dripping on his collar, and Leyna's long brown locks fared no better.

"A short respite, my lady. Drying us and our clothes. Then we move on. We must hasten." He shook his curled fists at his side for emphasis. "I have a purpose and I must not miss my—" Vygeas stopped his mouth tight, shutting down on the word *mark*.

Drostan hugged the granite boulder close, his entire front connecting with the rock. But it had not been enough. Or, perhaps, his skill not yet fully perfected in one so large and wilful. He grunted. The beast had wrenched control back as the daggers sank in. Pain had broken the bonds of the enchantment. Drostan sighed, releasing himself from his source.

"Who would have known Lady Leynarve of Monsae was skilled with throwing knives?" Drostan straightened his coat. "Where had the young noblewoman been these past five years since the demise of her parents? Or rather, with whom had she kept company?"

The warrior sages did not teach noblewomen the skill of knife throwing. Not even those who would learn advanced martial arts under the instruction of a warrior sage. It was usually the weapon of choice of brigands and thieves.

Drostan groaned. "Now I must seek another way." Clenching his fists, he hastened to his horse. He must not lose sight of them! "My course of action requires a more direct approach."

Ten

Closer to Eilean

Vygeas led them deeper into the forest. Their boots padded on the pine needle covered ground and Vygeas' boots squelched with each footfall. Leyna was correct and he allowed a slight nod— They did need to dry themselves before travelling further. He required dry feet at least. Dräger panted a soft nicker as he led him, followed by Leyna and Aiden. The late afternoon sunlight peeked through the tree canopy, lighting the path in blotchy sunlight, and dimming the further they progressed into the forest.

"We'll stop at the clearing ahead." Vygeas pointed to a roughly circular space, that separated an otherwise dense forest.

Vygeas tied Dräger's reins to a tree and cut a low branch with his dagger. In the centre of this gap in the tree growth he swept away the pine needles covering the forest floor with his makeshift broom.

"We shall make our fire here where it has less chance to catch the branches aflame."

Aiden began to scrape away the pine needles with his boot while Leyna cut a branch and assisted Vygeas to clear the forest floor. They left an area by the base of the tree trunks and not too far from where they would set the fire. Here the soft pine needles would make a comfortable bed.

Aiden and Leyna helped him to collect dry wood, ensuring they had longer thinner pieces to stake their garments. He arranged the firewood and lit it while Aiden tended to Dräger.

"My lord, I have seen no grass for your horse." Aidan placed the saddle and saddlebags underneath a tree.

"There are oats." Vygeas pointed to the bags. "It will have to suffice for this night."

The lad smiled and rummaged in the bags for the oats and a feedbag. Leyna shed her sodden leather armour, revealing a wet linen shirt beneath.

"We will stake our clothes to dry." Leyna removed her boots and grimaced. "Ugh. I have wet socks." She removed her socks and pulled a wide shawl from the bag she always hung on a long strap over her shoulder. "Do not look." Leyna flicked a glance his way and Aiden looked up at her command.

Vygeas dropped a medium-sized short branch on the fire then turned his back.

"Avert your eyes, young man." Vygeas made a spinning gesture with his hand and the lad faced the other way.

Wet cloth slipping off moist skin sent a warm swirl of human body heat, and Leyna's distinctive perfume, his way.

"Very well, you may turn around now." Leyna stood with her wide shawl wrapped around her body. Her shoulders, and her legs from mid-thigh down, were bare.

Vygeas glanced at her and then averted his eyes once more. It only required seconds. Her shapely thighs and slender arms were now an indelible impression on his memory.

"Well, I have no shawl, so it will only be boots and coat for me." Vygeas stripped off his sodden hooded grey coat and removed his boots then placed his coat and socks on the makeshift clothesline. Vapours rose from their clothing arranged on stakes beside the now roaring fire. The shirt Vygeas still wore steamed, and the heat soaked through to his skin, warming cold tired muscles.

Aiden walked across to the fire and lifted a foot to remove a boot.

"Hunter." Vygeas sat on the soft ground beside the fire and addressed Aiden. "What have you seen to catch for our supper this night?"

"Very little, my lord."

"Then you must become more observant, my young knave." Birds nested in the trees on their inward journey. Squirrels jittered and scampered through the trees to their night's resting places. Also, the many pad falls of a fox, a vixen and her cubs, as they made their way to their den, reached Vygeas. "Ye may find a pigeon or two nested back the way we came."

"Aye, my lord?" Aiden swallowed. "I must climb the tree?"

"I have food." Leyna picked up her bag. "Save the boy. It has been an exhausting day." Leyna brought dried meat wrapped in muslin from her bag.

Hmm. She had held *that* to herself.

Leyna unwrapped the dried meat and laid it before him. "We shall divide it between us."

Aiden sat close beside Vygeas next to the fire. He focused on the meat, tearing strips off his portion and chewing. Vygeas chuckled. The lad exerted great effort to keep his eyes averted from the barely clad young woman.

Indeed. So did he.

"Do you trust me now?" Leyna enquired as she passed more meat portions to himself and Aiden.

Vygeas faced Leyna, skittering his gaze over her chest on his way to her face. Leyna's cleavage showed an inch above the shawl. There was no seductive aura surrounding her, so she had not positioned her makeshift garment on purpose. Her state of dress, or lack of it, was purely out of the need for dry clothing. He swallowed.

"I beg your pardon, my lady."

"You must admit, I saved your life today." Her tone held conviction.

"Aye, Leyna and I thank you once more."

Leyna's scent was still hesitant, and a mild crease lined between her brows.

"Leyna, I assure you, your trust in me is not misplaced. I will do all in my power to ensure our journey is a safe one." Vygeas nodded for emphasis.

Two crooked teeth pressed on her lower lip. Uncertainty hinted its presence.

"What more can I say? You *must* doubt me not, my lady, or go your own way."

"You wish to part company?" Her tone was curt.

"No, but I wish for a travelling companion who...och. Ye are correct. It *has* been a hard day." He raised his hand, gesturing for the conversation to cease.

Leyna sat facing the fire, munching. Vygeas did the same. The venison was rich and gamey, but his jaw ached with the chewing. Aiden gnawed hungrily on his portion.

"We cannot travel further this day." Leyna announced. "It is now dark."

Vygeas bit hard on the venison. She was right. Once more. It was too late to start out again.

Vygeas awoke, sunlight angling low filtered through the tree branches, and wood doves gave their morning call. He stretched and shook off the stiffness in his muscles. Leyna and Aiden stirred. Leyna made them turn away once more while she dressed. Vygeas' socks were dry and only the hem of his coat damp. After kicking dirt over the coals of the fire, Vygeas walked Dräger out of the forest. Leyna and Aiden followed in silence.

Rain covered the road ahead of them, a light drizzle clearing as the morning wore on. A bank of cloud hovered over the nearby terrain, high hills that flattened to a green grassland as they neared the coast. The lad slumped along beside Vygeas.

"Here." Vygeas wiggled his fingers, indicating for Aiden to come beside Dräger. "Ye can ride him today for a wee bit."

Aiden's mouth dropped open. Closing it and standing taller, he put his knee on Vygeas' laced hands and Vygeas boosted him onto the still damp saddle. The lad beamed as he grabbed the reins.

"Och, no. I'll have those." Vygeas took back the reins and led the stallion, recommencing their walk.

"That's kind of you, Vygeas," Leyna whispered up to his ear, standing on her tiptoes to get there.

Vygeas blinked as a warmth filled his chest, sparked by her seeming approval. And her familiarity. And maybe even her trust.

"So, what is your true reason for going to Eilean?" Leyna cocked her head and looked out the corner of her eye at him. "For your urgency tells me you are pressed. And you seem too wise a man, sell-sword, to hurry to a battle."

"I, also, am intent on the merchant-mark in Eilean." He risked letting her know the truth.

Well, he'd not give it all away. And a little truth may nurture her confidence in him.

Leyna paused slightly, then picked up the pace once more. "So, you're a sell-sword-turned-assassin now? Why the new direction?"

"I owe our friend, Lord Ciarán, a debt."

Leyna raised her eyebrows.

No. He'd have to give her more than that. He straightened his shoulders and leaped in.

"I rebelled against his orders, was arrested, and I must win his *game*, as you put it, to secure my freedom. Or it's the gallows for me."

"Oh." Leyna stopped walking. Vygeas turned around to her. A strained expression crossed her face and sorrow's grey shadow emanated from her. Was she sad at the thought of him strung up, or a memory of someone else?

She recommenced her stride and double-timed some steps to catch up. Vygeas' heart started its thudding again as she neared, and he wiped his sweaty palms on his breeches.

How does she do that to me?

"But I have decided that when I kill the merchant, I shall get his wealth and give it to his workers." He finished with a nod.

"Oh, that's a brilliant idea." She turned a smiling face to him. The sweet rosy-scent of admiration poured from her but then it ceased abruptly. "You still intend to kill him?"

"Of course."

"He has a wife and children." She paused and turned her gaze to the road ahead, her mouth tight. "But you'll have fierce competition."

"Aye, but you know I have an advantage." He cocked an eyebrow and the corner of his mouth tried to follow it, but the scar snagged it, as usual.

"Hmm, tell me about that." It was a command. Couched in feminine softness, but a command all the same.

"Vygeas?" Leyna said when he hadn't answered.

"Aye, my lord. How *do* you do it?" Excitement and wonder oozed from Aiden. "You're so fast. You—" Aiden stopped short at Vygeas' glare.

"I think you owe it to us. Please tell what you do when you fight." Leyna's arm brushed against his hand, leaving traces of her warmth through his glove, and her scent rising to his nostrils.

Distracting.

"No, what you do all the time," she continued. "We are your team, after all

"Team?"

"Aiden and I will assist you in ...dealing with the merchant."

Vygeas raised his eyebrows and formed the word with care. "No."

"Aye. Eilean will be crawling with assassins. Someone's got to watch your back."

"I'm verra capable of seeing to my own back." His commoner accent had slipped through once again. Maybe Leyna wouldn't notice. "You need not be there."

"We'll help you," she insisted.

Determination came from her very pores and beat against his face. Vygeas gritted his teeth, as at times his *gift* was more of a curse.

"Besides," Leyna said. "I need to find my assassin. I can't do that if I'm not *there.*"

Aiden stirred in the saddle and Dräger flicked his head, tack jingling. "And—"

"No!" Vygeas shared his glare between them. "It will be too dangerous."

"I was going there anyway, if you remember?"

"You're a grown woman." He looked at those wide brown eyes in that perfect oval face. "You can be as reckless as ye want."

Vygeas turned to the lad in the saddle. "But you are my charge and I'll not put ye in harm's way. I planned on you minding Dräger by the coast and I would walk over to the island at low tide. Are ye hearing me?"

"Aye, lord. I hold your horse." Disappointment and humiliation mixed, and a dirty brown-green cloud floated from the lad.

He resumed their march. Bird song from a nearby rowan copse flitted across their path and the sighing of the wind in the pine trees that lined the road raised its voice overhead. The emotions of his companions swirled around—beside him and within him. He couldn't risk the lives of these two. Aiden, a perceptive, smart lad who would one day be a wise man.

And Leyna. She stirred his heart like none other since Elyse. He couldn't risk love again. Much is asked of those who love. So much to lose once you have it.

The heat of their vexation radiated from either side of him. Dräger pranced and Vygeas held the lead reins tighter, but both Leyna and Aiden remained quiet.

"Och! I got my heightened perception from a sorcerer, so I'd have the advantage over all those noblemen-warriors! There. Now you know." His brow tightened.

"Wow!" Awe came from Aiden.

Leyna smiled crookedly. Vygeas couldn't decipher what came from her.

"I knew it would be something like that," she said. "It seemed supernatural."

They walked in silence for a while. They had not recoiled at his revelation and the tightness between his shoulders relaxed. He gazed ahead where a tall single standing stone sat beside the road, its sharp edges worn over the years since its placement there. Soft swirls, carved deep, decorated the upper section and runes spoke their words beneath. The surrounding ground was flat and devoid of forest except for the trees, which skirted the edge of the field behind it.

Standing stones always evoked awe, and even fear, in those who approached them.

Vygeas sensed none in his companions.

Strange. He sensed *nothing*.

"Veee!" Leyna's scream tore his vision away from the standing stone ahead. A dark arm from a black-robed form wrapped around her chest and dragged her away from him, speeding her to the standing stone. Leyna and the dark form seemed to fly in the stone's direction, skimming across the distance to the rock-sentinel.

Drostan! *And the mage has blocked my gift with his magic.*

Armed with a sword, Drostan dragged Leyna away at speed. Vygeas ran, legs pounding, and his attention never leaving Leyna and her captor. She grabbed for her short sword, mouth set in determination, but in Drostan's restraining arm, she fumbled, and it fell to the ground.

"Let her go, Drostan!" Vygeas yelled, drawing his broadsword from over his shoulder and his dagger from its belt-sheath. The surge of energy and clarity that always accompanied a fight now emerged from his core.

Holding his broadsword in one hand was probably not his best idea. But with his gift dulled he needed everything to fight this mage.

Dräger shrieked.

"Grab the reins, Aiden!" Vygeas threw the command over his shoulder. "Get control of him."

Vygeas turned back to Drostan who held Leyna before him, her body blocking the mage's while he grasped her to himself. Eyes on Vygeas, Leyna nodded a fraction, giving permission.

Lifting his heavy broadsword in a feint, he jabbed at Drostan's face close above Leyna's head with his dagger in his left hand. Drostan's broadsword came up and deflected. Keeping it away from Leyna.

So, he didn't want her harmed. Just wanted to *take her*.

Not going to.

Vygeas side stepped to the left and thrust again. Drostan twisted, and Leyna wrenched herself free, moving away

"Run!" Vygeas didn't spare her a glance. His broadsword descended with all his one-handed might to Drostan's chest. Drostan lifted his sword up. He held it in a firm grip with both hands and blocked Vygeas' blow. Their swords slid to the hilts, the air screeching as metal scraped metal. Vygeas held the point of Drostan's blade away from himself with his dagger.

Face to face, Drostan's breath hit Vygeas and sweat beaded on the mage's forehead. Vygeas' lip curled. He had the advantage in physical strength, gift or no'.

"Did you enjoy your incarceration?" Drostan's words strained through his effort to hold Vygeas at bay, but a satisfied sneer emerged as he spoke into Vygeas' face.

Vygeas narrowed his eyes but didn't respond. A swirl of ache rose from the deep, the closeness of the man dragging up emotions from their mutual past, catching his breath, stuttering his heart.

Vygeas stepped back and centred his balance, then threw his dagger aside.

No close-up conversations!

He gripped his broadsword with both hands and brought it up to his shoulder. Twisted his grip out and brought the sword around in a tight arc and descended again on his close-quartered opponent. Metal clanged and Drostan's arms jolted.

Vygeas lifted his weapon high and central, readied for a downward cut, his long blade loomed threateningly, as did his own stance.

"Do you know who she is?" Drostan adjusted his grip. "She's *Lady* Leynarve *of* Monsae." A smirk sat on Drostan's face, and the man stepped back, moving closer to the solid rock behind him.

Vygeas' chest thundered. Not just from the excitement of the fight.

"The daughter you should have killed, assassin." Drostan spat the words.

Vygeas' throat constricted. Dräger neighed a short way behind him.

"Get her out of here, Aiden!" He kept his eyes on Drostan. Light footsteps approached from behind and Drostan's eyes widened.

"Leyna. Go!" It would be her.

"But I can fight." Her voice was a behind him. *Too close!*

"Go!" he growled. "He wants *you*. Leave! Now!"

Dräger's hoof-beats came closer, then a grunt, and the horse galloped off. Drostan's lips tightened.

"Does she know you murdered her parents?" Drostan stepped forward, sword point lowered at Vygeas' belly. Vygeas stepped aside, pushed Drostan's blade away, unsettling Drostan's balance. He slammed his elbow into Drostan's face for good measure. Drostan staggered to the standing stone, balance regained. His smirk broadened beneath a bloodied nose.

Vygeas snorted. Every battle is won or lost in a warrior's mind. Drostan was using an age-old tactic, trying to unsettle him.

It will not work.

Vygeas stepped in, circling his arm back preparing for a cutting blow with his full weight behind it.

The fool hadn't moved his back from the stone.

"I hope you're not falling in love with her. I *can* destroy her too." Drostan seemed taller by that stone.

Vygeas' mind clamped down with a gauntleted fist on what would rise from his past, tickled forth by the mage's words. He wielded his sword with all his might and connected his blade to Drostan's. The blow jarred to Vygeas' shoulders.

Drostan disengaged and lunged, then Vygeas stepped back. Drostan began an arc to pound him.

What! *Does Drostan draw strength from that standing stone?*

Vygeas let the blade slide down Drostan's sword, then snapped a blow with his right fist. The man had a hard chin but soft lips. They now matched his nose. Drostan wore a bloodied grimace. Vygeas blocked the next three thrusts and cuts from Drostan. He stepped around his enemy, luring him away from the sentinel in the centre of the field. He pushed him with downward cuts and backed him to the trees. Vygeas' arms burned, and his breath came hard.

Drostan's arms now shook with every connection of swords. Sweat trickled down his ruddy face and his shoulders heaved.

Away from that rock, Drostan is weaker.

Vygeas pushed.

He cut, thrust, stepped—forced his enemy back. Kicked, punched, trod, then pommelled Drostan's shoulder with his sword handle. Vygeas pressed his foe until Drostan stumbled his way into the edge of a nearby copse of oak.

Vygeas swung his sword in an arc either side of his body. Travelling wide, his blade would be sure to intimidate the mage.

Sword now held aloft and directly over his old acquaintance, Vygeas chopped down hard.

Drostan gathered strength from nowhere, scampering out of the way. The sharp tip of Vygeas' sword nicked Drostan's arm and tore a line of black cloth and flesh down to the wrist. Drostan yowled in pain, grasped his arm, and fled.

Vygeas followed through trees and tangled undergrowth. He slashed them aside with his broadsword as they clawed at his legs and impeded his pursuit.

In seconds, the evil-cloaked mage had gone.

Disappeared.

Vygeas heaved for air. A sting of pain came from the nick to his collarbone...and his knuckles where is gloves had torn...and his forearm. His throat burned and his sweat-soaked shirt stuck to his skin beneath his leather chest-armour.

He sought Aiden and Leyna on Dräger. They were far off.

The distant sounds had come back to him. He turned in a circle and sought Drostan. The mage was nowhere, and his senses had returned to their usual strength. He strained harder.

No. No Drostan.

It wasn't the last of him, for he wanted Leyna.

Lady Leynarve of Monsae. The one and only heir to the lands and title of the House of Monsae.

Daggers and double-sided bloody battle-axes! Why did she have to be *her!*

Drostan did not desire her. This reeked of Lord Ciarán.

"Oh," he said to the quiet forest he found himself in.

Not her, but the rights to her army.

A squirrel scurried up a tree, stopping frozen-still, claws in bark, every few steps, to ensure Vygeas hadn't moved. An acorn dropped to the ground with a *plonk*.

Vygeas rubbed his forehead so hard it was sure to leave a mark. So, it *was* true. Her parents his marks of years ago, and she the young lass he couldn't kill. But could he keep it from her?

"*Should* I keep it from her?" He dropped his hand. "And what of our...*companionship* if I do?"

Vygeas sighed then left the forest and ambled to the road. In the distance, Dräger faced him with two riders on his back. Concern and curiosity came at him in droves. Landing hard on the ground, he sat and waited for them.

He needed time to think.

ELEVEN

DROSTAN

Drostan sheathed his sword and pressed the long slice in his arm, only able to hold the top of the wound closed. Blood dribbled from his nose, joining that of his split lips and filling his mouth with a copper flavour. He spat.

Deamhan take that Vygeas. The *murtair* was a good fighter, even without his heightened senses.

"Ha! He never required the *gifting*." Drostan's exclamation misted around him as the cooling late afternoon air hit his breath. "That would have changed things—especially for the beautiful Elyse."

Drostan ground his teeth and leaned against a tree trunk. Elyse had spurned him. Shown the depth of her love for Vygeas. Wasn't a mage good enough for her?

Nae. Those clan lands in Dál Gaedhle hated mages. A long lingering abhorrence from the Dragon Wars of so long ago. The necessity of that secret cave outside the village a testament to their despising.

What a fool I was to think she would accept me...And a fool she made of me.

So simple to ease the pain in magic's power.

He snorted a short laugh. That Vygeas was so ambitious he gave all for the promised prowess.

Selfish man. *Glioc! Fool!*

And he believed I would do it? Torture her forever in an eternal hell?

Ifrinn! Hell, who did Vygeas think I was then?

Throwing himself into study and magic on the Isle of Innesfarne soon after had cut all ties with that tiny hamlet. Only on his employ as Lord Ciarán's mage had he finally discovered what had become of Vygeas.

Drostan pressed tight to his wound. Aye, the lad had gone a wee bit crazy, or so they had said. Learned his art and signed up as a sell-sword. Caught the eye of Lord Ciarán—unfortunate for him—and the lord had made him an assassin. Secret kill assignments. *Showed a natural talent.* A careless attitude for his own existence and a sharp eye for the best way to finish another's.

But now this recent reluctance to follow through on Lord Ciaran's murderous orders in battle…The assassin softening then?

Well, this mark on Eilean will bring him back to his senses. Unless he becomes besotted with his attractive travelling companion and seeks a redemption of some kind, witnessed by the Lady Leynarve of Monsae herself. For it *was* surely her.

Hmm. And now Lord Ciarán knows Vygeas is the very reason she remains alive—an uncompleted hit. *Before my time but now the man is found out.*

Drostan lifted himself away from the tree and staggered. Squirrels scurried up trees and roe deer leaped out of his path. One thing was certain—he'd been a fool. Divide and conquer through those nightmares had taken no effect. He had not counted on them both being too reticent to talk. Leaves on low branches whipped his bloodied cheeks as he brushed past. His enchantment skills to manipulate a large animal required improvement and grabbing Lady Leynarve had been futile. Drostan's brow tightened, and he swallowed blood.

He'd underestimated.

Never assume, a warrior sage would say.

Two things Drostan recalled. A healer sage lived nearby in these woods. Very well, he would endure the scarcity of rock, for he required assistance. Then he would aim for the coast where there was a cave—blessed sanctuary.

Drostan forced himself along the path, his sword scabbard *clunking* against tree trunks. Three things he would do and do them well. Use *his* gift to track that assassin. Stir up Vygeas' world and smash his plans against rock. Then fulfil his master's command and bring home the prize.

Leyna stood on the shore next to Vygeas. Aiden held Dräger's reins, scuffing his feet in the sandy ground. Way out from shore lay the ocean. Far ahead. So far ahead, the exposed seabed was now like a desert, the rippled sands extending before her as far as she could see.

"So, where's the water?" Aiden screwed his eyes to slits.

"The tide is out," Leyna said.

In the middle of the wide expanse of wet sands, within walking distance, was the small island of Eilean. Green shrubbery skirted the edges nearest its rocky coast. Rising high above and sitting on the highest peak of this mountain-island, sat a sandstone caisteal, built on the very bedrock. Tall turrets dominated at strategic points along the curtain wall. A long roof, belonging to the Great Hall of Worship, was the length of the uppermost section of the caisteal precinct. Dwellings clustered at the base of the outer bailey wall. Below this, and viewed through the archway of the town gate, people milled around a square and walked back and forth between market stalls sheltered by bright canvases.

Vendors packed up as the day neared an end. A smile tugged at Leyna's mouth. Mama had brought her here when a child, for a treat, this market known for its exotic goods. She had run up before Mama on the cobblestone road that started at the beach and snaked its way through this square and up to the caisteal.

Birdsong came from the trees, bringing her back to the now. Forest birds settled for the night, while seagulls squawked their way to their nests near the shore.

Seashells dotted the beach and tiny crabs scuttered sideways along the damp sands while the strong scent of kelp blew across from seaweed abandoned by the tide. Leyna's chest tightened. As a child she had played on a beach near to where they stood, building caisteals of sand and knocking them down before the white crested waves rode in and trampled her shell-decorated towers. Memories rolled in and crashed against her. Leyna let them buffet and float past on the evening breeze blowing off the distant waterline.

"Aye," Vygeas nodded. "I have heard you can view all from the mainland's shore." He broke the silence of Leyna's reverie. Vygeas pursed his lips and tilted his head to Leyna. "I could walk it."

"No, you cannot. Not now. You need to recover and the tide's coming in." Leyna's gaze wandered over Vygeas and rested on his torn gloves and raw knuckles, a cut in his forearm, and the blood seeping through his shirt at the collar.

"That merchant could sail soon, and I miss the chance." Vygeas lifted his brow. "The other assassins may already be—"

"The *tide* is coming *in*. You don't want to be there when that wall of water surges in."

"I'll hire a boat."

"You can't sail or row in the swell. You must wait till it's fully in and then cross. That will be well after dark." Leyna placed her hand on her hip. "You can afford a rest, some food to sustain you and those wounds need some attention."

"I've had worse."

"I'm sure you have."

Dräger nickered impatiently.

"What will you do with him?" Leyna flicked her thumb toward Vygeas' stallion.

"We'll go find somewhere to camp and a place for Aiden to wait for us." Vygeas nodded to the boy.

He is so good with the lad.

"Aye," Aiden sighed. "I mind the horse."

"Vygeas is right, Aiden. It's too dangerous for you. Dräger is valuable and we'll need him for our escape."

Vygeas muttered under his breath.

"Aye, master assassin?" Leyna turned to the scowling warrior.

"Let's just find this camp and some food." Vygeas said. "I need to be ready to go the moment that tide is fully in."

A row of stone houses and shops abutting the road that ran before the shoreline comprised the small village on the coast. It sat next to the long pier, which jutted out into the sandy seabed, its high pylons now exposed with the receded tide. Vygeas gave her coin and she bought bread, cheese, and dried meat at the shops before the vendors closed for the day. She and Aiden followed Vygeas as he led Dräger and searched through the forest on the outskirts of the village until he found a suitable campsite location in a circle of trees with a bare patch of earth and sky for a roof above them.

Vygeas had resumed his taciturn frown and returned to his usual pensive self.

So different from when he fought with Drostan. Fear had heightened her own senses. From the moment Vygeas' hazel stare had spoken to her, asking if he could risk it, she had only taken her eyes off him to pick up the weapons.

Fast and strong and skilled, Vygeas had moved with grace—flowing energy. The sword was the man, and the man was the sword.

Beautiful.

Shivers coursed along her shoulders and down her arms.

But Vygeas had sent her away. That still smarted. He maintained the mage was after *her*.

A chill tickled her spine.

She shook it off and unwrapped the food from the cheesecloth then set it out while Aiden tended to Dräger and Vygeas collected wood and set a fire, which soon blazed.

She ate the bread and cheese, the flames warming her against the chill evening.

"That mage isn't following us, is he, V? You'd be twitchier if he was." Leyna directed her question to the side of Vygeas' face, her heart warming at her own familiarity with him.

Vygeas stared into the flames as he placed the last piece of cheese in his mouth and chewed, but his senses were elsewhere. She could tell when he cast his senses out, seeking whatever, wherever he could. Vygeas looked across to her, the lambent light of the flame glowing on the sharp angles of his face.

His strong, handsome face. But more so, Leyna sensed the man that shone out of that face. How could Vygeas be a sell-sword? He seemed such a good man—albeit a little tortured.

"You knew that mage?" she asked. "Drostan, wasn't it?"

Vygeas' lips pressed tight. Emotions crossed his face like the cloud shift over the mountains they'd left behind. He blinked and his shoulders rose and fell; the collar of his shirt now red-soaked. Leyna ignored his silence and stood to reach for her bag.

"I need to look at your shoulder wound. It hasn't stopped bleeding." There were bandages in it somewhere. Behind her, Vygeas' fingers tapped his thigh.

"Take off your leather chest armour and we'll see about that wound." Leyna turned and placed the bandages on a flat stone, then went to the fire and removed a pan of water, which had boiled for tea. Leyna turned. Vygeas remained seated, staring at her.

"I know about wounds." She placed the pan next to the bandages. "Believe me, I've tended enough."

Vygeas' throat worked, then he undid his leather jacket to reveal a shirt soaked with blood down the left side.

"My lord, I wish to sleep—are you all right, my lord?" Aiden spoke behind her.

"I'm fine, lad, ye go sleep. The *healer* will attend me." Vygeas attempted his usual half smile. It always ended as almost a grimace but there was a playfulness in the expression.

Aiden walked back to his post near Dräger and made a bed for himself using the saddle for a pillow and was soon asleep.

Leyna turned back to Vygeas. He had removed his shirt, and his broad muscled chest glowed in the firelight. Clotted blood had dried as it dripped down the left of his torso and smudged where his shirt had dragged. Leyna swallowed. A scar from a previous wound ran deep and high over Vygeas' right shoulder. A round ragged scar near his hip, at the line of sinew, drew her eye to the arch of his hip, pointing out the line that curved downward. Leyna tore her eyes away and focused on the cloth in her hand.

She rummaged in her bag and brought out the small, wrapped package she sought. Taking out a generous pinch of the white granular substance, she threw it into the pan of hot water, and swirled.

"So, you're a healer sage?" The words were gruff.

"No. Not a sage. Far from it. I grew up near the sea. Saltwater is the best thing for healing wounds." Leyna dipped a corner of a clean cloth into the pan of saltwater, then dabbed at the cut that had nicked the muscle between shoulder and neck. Vygeas flinched.

"Aye, the salty water stings at first but it cleans. Be brave, sell-sword."

Vygeas looked at her from beneath his eyebrows and squinted as she continued cleaning his wound. She dabbed the deepest section and his jaw muscles tightened.

"It won't need sewing." Leyna cleaned the rest of the blood from his chest, her hands trembling as she wiped clots and smears away from his firm, taut abdomen.

"Humph." Vygeas' eyes never left her.

She pressed a clean folded cloth directly onto his injury and wound a bandage around his shoulder and under his arm, over and over.

Leyna stood close, the warmth rising from Vygeas' body sent her heart going—again. What was it with this quiet, serious man? This *honest* sell-sword. He seemed at odds with his profession, though. And there was a goodness in him...unlike her recent companions. She could let herself fall in love with him.

Her hands fumbled with her acknowledgment of it, threatening to tangle her fingers in the bandage. She finished wrapping his shoulder then lifted her hands away from Vygeas and turned to tidy the things back in her bag. Anything to not be facing him and have him read her thoughts. Her heart picked up its tempo. *Can he read thoughts?*

What she felt for Vygeas was inexplicable. Undeniable and without reason. *Or sense*. Leyna threw the unused bandages into her bag. Was Vygeas a man with whom she could spend this life? She blinked at her inward question. She'd only just met him. How could she be asking herself such a thing?

Leyna stepped out of the circle of the firelight and threw the remaining saltwater out on the ground and huffed. Mama had believed in love at first sight. Was it a true thing after all? She had come to love Robbie, but that was after some time and very much out of convenience.

This man was something different altogether.

Leyna spun back to the fire. Vygeas stood in front of her, her face at the height of his bare chest. She tilted her head back. Vygeas gazed at her, his features unusually soft. A slight curve edged his lips. His eyes looked directly into hers, as if he'd heard her inner turmoil.

"You're conflicted. I am too. But..." Vygeas shrugged his good shoulder a little, his mouth curving to a smile—as much as it could with that scar—then it relaxed as he leaned in close.

Leyna didn't pull back. On her mother's grave, she should have. But she couldn't. Vygeas' eyes mesmerised her, his face descending to hers. She kept her eyes open, and his hot mouth covered hers. She shut her eyes then, savouring the sensation of this man so close. Leyna's body pressed to his as his uninjured arm came around her waist to her back and pulled her into him. Leyna didn't resist. She didn't want to. She only wanted this.

And him.

TWELVE

IN THE FIRE'S GLOW

Vygeas' lips surrounded her own. He pressed his mouth hard to hers, matching his firm muscled body against her length. Vygeas' contact was one long question as his lips moved from hers and traced a gentle journey across her face and her neck. Shivers rose, peaking with every fresh contact Vygeas' mouth made with her skin.

Vygeas' hand moved from Leyna's back, and she leaned into his warmth, holding her body in place close against his. His fingers worked on the side-ties of her leather chest-armour. Warmth and desire swelled from within her, wanting more of this man's touch. She reached up and ran her fingers into his long hair and then pulled his head onto her chest, allowing his soft warm mouth to caress the skin of her exposed breasts. Her legs ached to entwine with his and... Leyna's breath caught in her throat.

Haven't I vowed I'd never use love for expediency ever again?

She'd aligned herself with Robbie for protection—aligning herself totally. Walking away from his hanging corpse she'd promised herself that in future love would be for love, not practicality nor convenience.

Vygeas halted his kisses and pulled back. He looked her in the eye—as if seeing through her heat to her thoughts.

"Very well." He stepped back.

Leyna blinked. He was behaving like a gentleman. Truly rare in the men she had found herself in the company of these past few years.

"No, I...it's not that...I just..." Leyna trailed off.

"You need not explain. I presumed too much." Vygeas moved away and sat beside the fire.

"No." She shook her head a little. "I like you."

Vygeas arched an eyebrow.

"But with your special ability you probably knew that already." Leyna pressed her top teeth onto her lower lip.

"I didn't need a gift for that, my lady." Vygeas glanced at her mouth and smiled.

"I don't want you to think...just because we are travelling together..." Leyna shuffled her shoulders slightly. "We need to get to know each other more, don't you think?" She straightened, standing taller with her resolve.

"Aye, my lady. But please come here and sit beside me so we can talk." Vygeas spread his coat, which he sat upon, and patted it with his hand.

Leyna stepped to him, counting the beat of her thudding pulse, willing it to slow. She focused on the conversation to be had, not the heat low in her belly. Nor Vygeas' bare torso and the lingering warmth from his lips. She settled herself beside him on his cloak, her inner fire diminishing. Her bottom lip pinched where she chewed it. She released it and ran her tongue over her lips.

Vygeas inclined his head. "You go first, my lady." The scarred corner of his mouth puckered in that half smile. It was endearing in its own way.

"I am Lady Leynarve of Monsae," she said through a sigh. Leyna concentrated on his face and examined every nuance of his expression. He showed no surprise.

"You know?"

"Aye, and henceforth I shall call you Leynarve."

"Oh, please do not." She gave a cheeky grin.

"You can't stop me."

"But it will give away my identity."

He leaned close, placing his soft lips to hers. "Then I shall whisper it when we are in company." His face was inches from hers.

"How do you know?" Her words were husky. "About my title?"

"Drostan told me." He leaned back.

Leyna's throat tightened. "How does *he* know?"

"Drostan is Lord Ciarán's mage."

"The lord who wants the merchant dead?"

"The same one. He also wants you."

"Dead?" Ice shot through her.

"Nae. Lord Ciarán needs you alive, my lady. He wants your army, the one entitled to you as the Lady of Monsae, and which, if he married you, would be his by marital right."

The fire crackled, and a log popped, the heat of the flames bathed her in its warmth as that ice landed in her guts.

"Why did you leave your home, my lady?" Vygeas spoke low in her ear, his hot breath tickling her cheek.

"And don't call me *my lady*."

"Leynarve, tell me why you left lands and title."

Leyna's heart skipped a beat. He had spoken her full name once more. Warmth flowed right through her, chasing away the ice.

Maybe she *would* let him name her so.

"I was angry. I wanted nothing to do with it." She shook her head. "The title and responsibility had not protected my parents from danger. Why should I crave it? All I longed for was to kill the assassin responsible."

"How did you plan to do that?" Incredulity rang through his words.

Leyna sent him a sharp glance. "I had some training with a warrior sage, as you know. I'd received instruction as any noblewoman would. I couldn't be a warrior-woman, for, as my parents' only heir, I was to be the future Lady of Monsae. But I know enough. I'm determined."

"Determined enough to attack a sell-sword, with only a blunt short sword, while travelling alone?"

"It was a bad day." She gave a brief shrug. "I'm usually better than that."

"Ye will have to be or else ye will be dead, my Lady Leynarve of Monsae." Vygeas' index finger pointed at her nose. "Too confident in your own ability. It will get you killed."

Leyna held his stare. His face moved close once more, and gentle lips touched hers.

"Don't do it," he whispered, his breath caressing her face. "You'll be bettered."

Leyna dragged her gaze from his lips surrounded by short, dark whiskers.

Past the fire, lying beside the tethered horse, Aiden slept soundly. If only she was that age once more, with family alive, and all of life before her.

"I have been with thieves for the past five years." Leyna turned back to Vygeas who fixed his gaze on her. "We stole from wealthy lords, merchants, and bankers. Metal and stones were the only things worth the risk. The band were unsure of me at first but when they realised I have a *special gift*—" she arched a brow to him— "they kept me on."

Vygeas smiled. "And what is your talent, Leynarve?"

"I can find any way of escape. I helped them plan the thefts, and they kept me close in case something or someone blocked the pre-determined exit. I always found another way out if it was." The side of her mouth tugged.

"Beautiful and clever. Hmm." Vygeas leaned in and once more placed warm lips on hers.

Leyna let him.

"Your turn," she said when his lips finally left hers.

"I am an assassin and sell-sword as you know."

"With a unique talent." A thought came to her. "*Always* an assassin?"

"Always." Vygeas nodded. "With an advantage."

Always?

"Was Drostan the mage who gave you your gift?" she asked.

"Aye. Even before Drostan studied with the masters and learned the art of a mage, he would grant gifts. He already knew some magic and was powerful with it. He dwelled hermit-like in a cave outside of my village. He would grant your heart's desire—for a price." Vygeas remained silent for a time, chewing his lip in thought.

"What was your price?"

Vygeas' jaw muscle hardened.

"V?"

He sighed, it came from deep within him.

"V, what's wrong?"

"I had to perform a task before Drostan would grant me some special advantage. I said I would do anything, but what he had in mind I couldn't bear." Vygeas' eyes flicked up to hers and held her gaze. "My price was to kill the woman I loved."

"What?" Leyna's stomach tightened, all warmth dissipated, chased away by a stunned-cold. "Did you do it?"

Vygeas' expression tore his facial features. "I had no choice, Leynarve." His eyes pooled with tears.

"No choice!" Leyna flinched back from him. "Everyone has a choice!"

"You don't know how evil Drostan was. How evil he still is."

What! Vygeas didn't seem a man who would do such a thing—*And I've let myself feel for him*—Leyna made to stand.

"No, please stay. I need to explain to you. Trust me," he pleaded now.

The ache in Vygeas' voice kept Leyna on his coat beside him.

"Why?" Her words were barely a whisper.

"Once Drostan knew her, he wouldn't let her go. He gave me an ultimatum. *I* kill Elyse,"—Vygeas choked on her name— "or he would torture her for ever. I didn't care for my gift then. I just wanted her safe. So, I sent her to the grave with a peaceful death. I couldn't bear her suffering throughout all eternity."

"But you still *killed* her." Leyna couldn't keep the disbelief out of her voice.

"Truly, I regret it. I live with self-loathing. I was so stupid and selfish." Vygeas' self-disdain was plain on his face. "I never took a thought for the consequences. Ambitious desire blinded me. I would do anything to be better than *they* were. Better than any nobleman-warrior." Vygeas' hazel eyes were torn, tortured. Tears streamed down his solid cheeks and jaw. He blinked and wiped his face with his palm, turning his head away.

Leyna swallowed hard. The cold dissipated a little, replaced by an ember of understanding.

We all have demons to bear. This was his. This quiet man had held this raging secret for years. Had this driven him to becoming a ruthless assassin?

Was he? What she knew of this man didn't fit.

"So, you've killed, and you do so for money." Accusation rang through her tone.

Vygeas whirled back. "I only kill the deserving."

"The deserving?" Leyna snapped her words at him. "Your Elyse didn't deserve to die."

"I only took employment for those marks who oppressed the poor, who'd persecuted the weak and the helpless. And believe me, Leynarve, there are too many in this world." His voice was hard-edged, like his blade. "I love justice enough to die for it. I risked my life with every mark." Vygeas faced her, his tone changing. "Don't be so high and mighty with me. You're on a path that leads to the same destination."

"The man who killed my parents deserves to die."

"How do you know it was a man? There are women assassins also."

"I saw his cloak as he escaped through the window. He was leaving as I entered my parents' bed chamber." Leyna paused. "That's odd. I only remembered this after the dream the night before last." She swallowed, focussing on the campfire, and pushed hard against her memory to prevent her mind from recalling the rest of that nightmare.

The bright flames of the fire were dying to an amber glow as coals took over.

"This will be my last employ as an assassin and then I shall be free of Lord Ciarán." Vygeas looked into the coals also and spoke through gritted teeth. "I never wish to involve myself with that *deamhan* again."

"We both need a fresh start." Leyna placed her hand on his arm. It was warm and stirred the embers of her compassion, gradually replacing the chill. "Once I find and kill this assassin on Eilean, I shall move on also."

Vygeas bowed his head. "Och, no!" His voice was soft and overflowed with pain as his commoner accent surfaced. He struggled within himself. If only she had his ability to sense and know things. Vygeas' hands clenched and unclenched. He moved from her side and spun around to kneel before her.

"Leynarve." Vygeas reached out for her hands. Leyna offered them, and he held them in his large firm grip. She sat in silence and his intense gaze held hers captive. The world stood still while she waited for his words to match his intense expression.

"Lady Leynarve of Monsae, I beg your forgiveness. He deceived me. I discovered after the act that your parents were guilty of no injustice. Lord Ciarán had duped me. He wanted your father's army, and Lord Monsae would not comply with Lord Ciarán's ambitions."

Leyna's heart numbed. As numb as at her first realisation that her parents, her only family, lay dead in their bed—slain.

Were the words Vygeas had spoken real? The man remained immobile in front of her, his eyes never leaving hers. Loose hair fell over the warrior's shoulders; his eyes were moist, and a storm of emotions filled his face. Crazed his brow. Ripped at his scarred lip.

Guilt. Remorse. Self-admonition. Briefly they caught her attention.

"You?" Leyna's voice was a whisper.

Vygeas nodded, then bowed his head and remained so for some moments.

"You." Accusation filled her voice, now a little louder. The numbness left her, replaced by sensations, red and hot and spiralling upward. The hem of Vygeas' grey coat flitting out of her parents' bedroom window filled her mind's eye. She wrenched her hands from his and put them by her side. Rough material scrunched in her curled fist as she grabbed that same grey cloak, the very one on which she now sat.

Leyna jumped up and snatched her bag and short sword from where they lay.

"Leynarve?" Vygeas remained on his knees next to the fire.

She strode away from him.

"Leynarve!" His voice echoed around their campsite.

She quickened her pace as his footsteps came closer. She spun.

"Don't touch me!" She held her hand, palm out.

Vygeas stepped closer. Leyna drew her sword and pointed it at him. "Don't touch me, Vygeas," she growled.

Vygeas stood back, hands up in surrender. Hurt and self-abhorrence filled his expression. His chest heaved.

She didn't care *what* he felt. She clenched her jaw against acknowledging his pain.

"Leynarve. I need *your* forgiveness, so I can live with myself. Forgive myself."

"I...can't." Her words came through her ragged breath. She turned and ran. He followed her. "Stay where you are, Vygeas!" she shouted and spun, her sword-point at his chest.

Vygeas skidded to a halt, her blade tip touching his bare skin.

"Leynarve." Her name wrenched from anguish.

"My lord?" Beside Dräger, Aiden called through his sleepiness.

"Don't follow me." Her words cut the night.

She ran.

Thirteen

The Task Beckons

"My Lord Vygeas. The Lady Leynarve is leaving? My lord—?" Aiden rose from his saddle-pillow.

Vygeas' heart bounced against his ribs, pounding the ache and the numbness left by Leynarve's response. Her hurt, anger, and the stinging scent of betrayal receded into the forest where she ran, crashing into branches and stumbling over fallen logs.

The lad's questioning waves of concern reached him.

"Go after the lady." His order was sharp.

Aiden flinched, now thoroughly awake. "Aye, lord."

"Take Dräger. The lady needs a horse." Vygeas marched over to the saddle, plucked it from the ground and threw it on his stallion.

"Aye, lord." Aiden's voice strangled around his disbelief. "You wish the lady to have your war horse?"

"Lady Leynarve *must* be safe," Vygeas yelled, then pulled himself up. "Return her to me, please." He tightened the girth. "Hurry. I must leave here soon. The tide will be in, and I must obtain a boat and get to Eilean this night." Vygeas drew his short dagger from his right boot and handed it to the lad. "It may require sharpening. I recall ye can do that."

Aiden smiled, tucked the dagger into his belt, and jumped into the saddle, kicking the stallion to a gallop. The backs of lad and horse disappeared into the darkening night.

Vygeas stood in the silence, emptiness enveloping him.

"What a fool." His words tore his dry throat.

Vygeas grasped his hair above his brow with both fists and pulled tight. Had he expected it would be easy? That Leynarve would readily forgive him?

He who had slaughtered her parents!

"Missed the target! What a stupid wretch." Vygeas yanked harder on his hair, threatening to tear it from his scalp. How had he conceived there'd be hope for the likes of himself? Seeking absolution from his past. The reality of his victim's grief so close he'd reached out and touched it as it shrouded him. The hairs on his forearms still stood erect from her grief moving on to anger and then seething revenge, burning him with it.

How could one such as her forgive one such as I?

Vygeas dropped his hands, dragging a sigh from the depths of his being.

An owl called as the night awakened. Vygeas shook himself, then dressed in his leather armour and gathered his belongings together. He strapped his broadsword in its scabbard over his shoulder, flinching at the pain of his injury and bracing himself for his task on Eilean. He must get back to the village by the shore and hire a boat.

A horse's footfall crashed through the trees. Aiden's anxiety reached him first.

"Ye saw her, lad?"

"Aye but..." Reticence vibrated off him.

"Tell me," he ordered.

"I saw her. Spoke to her—"

"Where is she?" Vygeas still could not sense Drostan anywhere, but that meant nothing. Drostan could be out there blocking him. Seeking her.

"In the woods my lord—"

"Good. Can ye bring her back to me?"

"Um..." Aiden hung his head and fidgeted with Dräger's reins.

"Speak lad!"

"She will nae return with me, my lord. The Lady Leyna says she does nae want tae speak to ye. Well, she said more than that, but I dare not repeat it. 'Twas nae language for a lady, ken?"

"Go back to her. Keep her in the woods away from rock of any sort. Protect her. I don't need you. She does." Vygeas nodded his final command, slapped Dräger on the rump, and turned his face to Eilean.

It only took a short while to reach the village by the beach where they had purchased their stores that afternoon. The high tide had transformed the shore and the desert sands were now grey, deep sea, lapping the beach. The pier, which in the afternoon had sat comically high above wet sand, now echoed with the slap of water against its pylons and slatted walkway. Over the glittering water, sitting high in the night's horizon, stood the proud caisteal of Eilean, its gates and windows winked their torchlight. The night sky was also ablaze with its own twinkling lights.

Vygeas walked onto the pier and headed for the section with a sign that read *boats for hire*. A cool breeze stirred and played through his loose hair. He secured his hair in a leather thong and nodded his greeting to the man standing by the sign. Clouds gathered in the east and obscured the stars that hugged the horizon.

"So, ye have sailed afore?" The boatswain's query brought Vygeas out of his observations. The stocky man with a large greying beard loosened a thick rope looped around a post and attached to the small boat next to the pier. He eyed Vygeas' sword sitting proudly above his shoulder. Caution wafted over from him.

"Nae. Cannae be that hard. I'm only going from here to there." Vygeas indicated with his chin to his present position and then to the shoreline of Eilean.

"Och, aye then. Mind that the tide runs out in six hours, so if ye could return my wee boat on the next high tide that would be grand. Otherwise, I charge ye another day's hire, like." Bushy eyebrows raised above eyes black in the shadowy night. "Watch the weather too. There's some cloud far over there in the east, but it will surprise ye how quickly a storm comes upon ye in these waters, aye?"

"Thank you." Vygeas paid the man coin, took the rope from him, and stepped into the boat.

The wee rowboat rocked with his movement. Vygeas steadied himself, as if on Dräger, and the rocking settled. He sat on the bench in the middle of the small craft, picked up the oars and began to row. He pulled on the oars which dipped and splashed in the water. Saltwater hit his face, stinging his forearm and raw knuckles.

He would head straight for the cobblestone ramp at the far shore, as most travellers would. Nearing the island, he would row around to the southern side where he'd dock, away from anyone's view from the mainland, and nearer to the seaport where ships berthed. He gave a curt nod. That was his strategy. He'd have to stick tightly to it. The tide would pay him and his designs no regard.

But what were schemes worth?

He'd yearned to wipe the past, so he might be with the brave, feisty, accomplished woman he'd encountered. He may have had a chance. But those plans had gone awry.

This undertaking with Gille Fhialain *had* to succeed.

Dense forest surrounded Leyna. Cool touched her on every side as the darkness of night deepened and enveloped the trees.

"How dare he!" Leyna paced back and forth. "How dare Vygeas be *that* man. The assassin who…"

The one who had slaughtered my parents! She grit her teeth for the words could not come out.

How dare Vygeas also be a man she would consider for love.

"Why had I not disembowelled him the first day we met?" Leyna ceased her pacing. "Because I had no idea who he was then. I'd never have guessed I'd feel this way about him. Aargh!" Her cry wrenched out from between her teeth, misting around her face in the cooling night air.

Leyna slid into a squat against the trunk of the nearest tree, releasing the scent of its bark.

And he'd killed his past love. Leyna shook her head and shivered.

Then she trembled.

Unbelievable. Impossible. And he'd admitted it to her. *Both counts.*

What does he want from me? Forgiveness? Absolution?

Did he expect things to be the same after these admissions?

He had spoken of trust on their journey. How could she trust him knowing this?

Leyna gripped her upper arms and grunted. To be honest, even though she was angry at him—and she most definitely was—she couldn't deny her attraction.

She hugged herself tightly.

"Oh, I'm being a fool!"

It had been a broken man begging for forgiveness kneeling in front of her. Was it a new man with a heart changed? Had she met him on the cusp of transformation?

Why then was he on his way to Eilean? To complete a hit and kill a mark for his own freedom—leaving a merchant's family without a father and provider.

It made no sense.

To forgive him...made even less sense.

Her breath halted in her throat. But Vygeas was right. She also was on her way to kill...

Hooves pounded through the forest and a horse nickered. It was Dräger.

"What are you doing here?" Leyna stood, drawing her blade.

"Please, my lady, it is me. Aiden."

"Where is he?" Leyna peered past him.

"Lord Vygeas has gone to Eilean, my lady."

Leyna leaned back onto the tree, steadying herself, drawing long deep breaths. Dräger snorted softly.

"My lady?" Aiden's voice came through the dark night. "My lord said—"

"I don't care what your lord said," she spat at him.

The boy was quiet. Leyna's cheeks burned.

"Oh, I'm sorry, Aiden." She gentled her voice. "It's not your fault. What did your lord say?"

"That I was to protect you. Keep you away from rock and keep ye safe. He gave me his dagger." Aiden's hand rested on the hilt of the blade tucked into his belt.

"Ha! I don't need protecting." Scorn filled her tone. "Keep me from *rock*?"

"Aye, so we may as well go back to the fire by the edge of the forest. It still burns, and we can be safe and see people coming...and he's not there anymore."

Leyna leaned away from the tree. The breeze blew in the treetops of the forest surrounding her, a soft clatter like a burn running over boulders.

"Very well, young man, *protect* me if you must. Your company, and yours only, will be mine tonight." She paused before taking another stride. "I'm trusting you. This better not be a trick. He's actually gone, has he?"

"Truly my lady, I jest not." Under his breath he added, "I dare not."

Leyna's mouth tugged. Aiden was a good lad and would become a good man one day.

The walk back cooled her. The camp was empty, only coals burning low in the fire pit. Aiden went about placing smaller logs on the fire and stoking it. The wind blew it to life and soon the flames warmed her face and hands. She sat beside the campfire, the warmth penetrating her clothing and touching her skin.

"Why are ye mad at Lord Vygeas, my lady?" Aiden had done it again. The lad was a sage.

"He lied to me." Leyna's hand went to the handle of her short sword.

"May I ask how?"

"He slaughtered my parents." Leyna's throat thickened and her veins heated once more.

"But he would nae have done it if he knew you, my lady. I am certain of it. My Lord Vygeas is fond of ye. Hurting ye is the last thing he'd wish tae do." Aiden threw more wood on the flames.

"He killed them, and then asked me to forgive him." Leyna shook her head at the incredulity of the situation.

"Did you?" The lad stared straight at her. Innocence itself.

"No." Leyna couldn't hold the disbelief, nor the nastiness, from her voice. Aiden flinched.

The fire cracked and popped. The wind blew harder overhead, the treetops now sounded like an ocean. The flames of the fire blew horizontal.

"My mam always said—"

"I don't care what your mam said," she snapped.

Aiden sat motionless beside her, his lips tight.

"I'm sorry, Aiden. I'm angry at your lord and I'm taking it out on you."

"I forgive you, my lady." Silence followed and the young man held his hands out to the fire.

Moments passed. Aiden was unusually quiet. Leyna could bear it no longer.

"What did your mother say?"

"That ye must forgive."

"*Must* forgive? What did *she* know about it?" Derision laced her words. She pressed her mouth closed to prevent more hurtful tones.

"Bandits attacked my Da on his way home from his smithy forge one night. They killed him." Aiden's voice was thick. "Mam said we must forgive. Not for the bandit's sake, but for our own. Otherwise, it would eat us up and kill us inside."

Aiden sat quietly, peacefully. He'd just recounted his father's murder and he was at *peace*? Leyna let her stare remain on him.

"I know ye think it's daft." Aiden looked directly at her, his eyes moist. "A warrior sage caught them, and the judges hung 'em. But my mam said even if that had nae happened, we had tae release the hurt we felt from them, for what they'd done, so *we* could be free. Otherwise, we'd never be." Aiden gazed back at the fire. "So, one day, before Mam got sick, we all walked up to the top o' the ben just ootside our village. It's the first of the hills that line the glen that runs by the grand river, which flows out to the south ocean. The wind funnels through it, ye ken. We stood there—Mam, Bessie, Nan and Pop, and Uncle

Seaghán. And we threw it over. All our hate, hurt, and grievance against those bandits. The wind took it away, and we were free." He turned his head calmly and smiled.

Leyna double blinked, wrinkled her nose, and swallowed.

The wind gusted and the ocean in the treetops roared.

"We'd better find shelter." Her voice was lost in the wind and Dräger's alarmed neighing. She gathered the belongings and headed into the dense forest, Aiden leading Dräger behind him.

FOURTEEN

THE CAVE OF THE POWERS OF THE AIR

Wadded bandaging stiffened Drostan's arm and restricted his movement. The healer sage had applied a poultice after stitching the wound closed.

It was all taking too long. He ripped it off and demanded bandaging only. He had work to attend to.

The sage knew of the cave and provided directions. Not that he required them. Drostan headed where she pointed, and the sandstone called him. He followed its drawing, pulling him with a firm hand as he neared.

He reached a track at twilight. It led through a wood and arrived at a shingled beach. Moderate sized pebbles of pink, beige, and grey hues made up the shingle as they reflected the diminishing light of the setting sun. Salt air tingled his tongue and the crash of the high tide's swell on the shoreline was a constant rhythm as he tramped along the uneven pebbles to the cave mouth. He fetched the flint from his bag and struck it to light the torch left outside the cave entrance. Pulling the overhanging foliage aside from the cave mouth, he stepped through.

The torch flared to life and illuminated the large chamber. He edged the yellow-cream walls, keeping close to their seeping sides, for the whole bottom of the cave, except for a narrow lip of a walkway at the perimeter, was one deep, underground pond. A ceiling arched high above him; stalactites hung like great tree roots and dripped leisurely onto the clear deep dark water of the pond.

He trod to the back of the cave and stood on an out-cropping of rock that jutted over the pond.

"Ah." His satisfied tones echoed around the cavern. A rock divination bowl hewn by nature. "To work."

He stepped to the cave's wall and chocked the torch into place in a nook. He ignored the twinge that snaked down his arm from the injury and crossed again to the rock that protruded over the pond and stood.

Drostan quieted his mind and focused on the rock surrounding him.

His source and his conduit. His foundation. His all.

He drew from the natural podium beneath him. Stretching out his arms, he sought more from the cave's walls and ceiling. He would need all that his body and soul could bear for that which he had in mind. Delight ran through him. This cave was ideal, a gift from the land and the energies within it.

Power followed the delight. Like lightning's sting it slowly built, and with a flash it filled him. His body arched, his spirit filling with energy.

The pond illuminated, shining light behind closed lids. He opened his eyes to a panorama spreading before him. The Isle of Eilean stood shadowed at the far end of the pond, its torch lit caisteal proud on its heights and the village nestled below. The village on the mainland sat in the foreground of this three-dimensional scene.

Vygeas stepped onto its pier.

Drostan was not too late. Fate was in his favour this night. He inhaled deeply, concentrating hard and focussing on the air and Vygeas both together, and spoke from his spirit.

"O mighty powers of the air,
Water too, I bid you—care.
Thou who rulest over the seas,
Bring forth from thy dungeon, deep and dark,
Thy shackled prisoners now held in check.
Unleash thy winds.
Blow the world away!

"Surge, o ravenous seas.
Transport the ocean's might.
That which makes the bravest warrior tremble
And pale with fright.

"Release thy clouds, o spirit of the air.
Set them galloping free.
From their churning heart discharge thy bolts.
Boom thy lighted spear with rage.
Shower mine enemy with thy wrath.

Route him by thy storm this night.

Impale him on the craggy rock!"

The echoes of his summoning resounded throughout the cave and then died down.

All was still.

He stood on the podium, taking deep spiritual breaths. A force from the very elements of the universe itself surged through him. He yielded himself, imbued by it. His spirit drank of its wine and became drunk.

Drostan left his body and his spirit rose above the agitated waters of the underground pond.

The waves on the prow of the small craft thudded off-beat with each splash of Vygeas' dipping oars. Directly ahead, the Isle of Eilean sat in the late evening's rest, the narrow streets were empty of villagers now home for the night. Wisps of cloud skated past the caisteal flagpoles sitting proud on her turrets. A gust of wind pushed at the boat, nudging the nose to the left. He rowed more on the right to compensate. Spray hit his face on that side and stung an otherwise unknown cut from his clash with Drostan that very afternoon. So much had occurred since then, the altercation was all but forgotten.

Leynarve will be with Aiden.

Gusts of wind picked up a wave that doused the boat. Vygeas flinched at the frigid sea, now drenched by it. The wave left a puddle in the boat's belly. He shook water from his stinging eyes as cold trickled beneath his armour.

"Concentrate on the task at hand!" he reprimanded himself. "Leave thoughts of Leynarve to another time."

Vygeas flicked away the wet hair stuck to his face. To the west, a bank of dark grey cloud gathered and travelled in his direction at speed. Its denseness darkening the night sky further, casting a shadow in its path and blotting out the starlight. The wind roared across the water lifting the waves higher. A large surge of water pounded the side of his boat and almost tipped it. He held the oars tight as light flashed from the direction of the approaching storm clouds. Thunder gently rumbled in the distance.

Vygeas faced Eilean. Soon he would veer left and row around to the lee side of the island. Perhaps the approaching storm would not reach there with the harbour side shielded by the high mount of rock, the whole height of the island.

He rowed on and now the wind did the work for him, the boat veering left without his intentional steerage. He would have to row tight to keep the craft near the shore. Hug it around the edge of the island to reach the ocean side. And pray the wind and waves did not sweep him out into the ocean.

The boat rocked, bobbing up and down on the ever-increasing waves. Often his oar strokes did not touch the water. The wind pushed him further as water splashed into his mouth. Saltiness drew saliva from his tongue. He spat out seawater, unable to remove the taste.

Waves hit Vygeas side-on, broadsiding his small craft. He gasped. The waves were more than twice as high as he. He rowed vigorously to turn and ride into the waves head-on. Shoulder screaming, gloves torn, knuckles stinging. For a moment he faced west, cresting a breaker.

A lightning bolt brightened sea and sky around him, cutting the pier by the mainland in two. Blazing wood, charcoal, and a sharp scent he couldn't name, assailed his nostrils. The very air seemed to burn. Then his body shook, the surrounding waves vibrated, and the charred air trembled with the energy released from the thunderclap. Vygeas dropped his oars and covered his ears. The wall of sound would deafen him!

Soaring above the pool in the cave, Drostan's spirit hovered over the image of Vygeas.

The waves pounded Vygeas. He willed the winds to tear at him and to sink Vygeas to a deep, watery grave.

Waves crashed over the edge of the underground pond and the churning waters of the pool splashed the ceiling. Stalactites threatened to tear from their deep-rooted bases with the pounding.

Drostan smiled. The power surged and permeated him, exhilarating every fibre of his being.

The seething ocean swelled and tumbled around Vygeas. He rowed aiming for the shoreline of Eilean opposite the mainland. Palms bleeding.

Forget the plan!

A fierce wave smashed against the side of the small vessel, snapping that oar. He rowed on with one. Lightning flashed, jagged bolt after jagged bolt, illuminating the sky. Their thunders rumbled into each other. Vygeas' whole body vibrated to his core, and he shivered from the bitterly cold water, iced by the savage winds swirling from every direction. He sensed the way ahead, only glimpsing it through blinding flashes of lightning. The wee boat dipped and rolled as he held the sides, showered by torrential rain. A wave jolted his slippery bloodied hand and dragged the other oar into the surging sea.

He wiped the salty rain from his eyes and tried to focus. He was far from a seasoned sailor, but this was no natural storm. He searched, peering through his rain-swept vision, straining his thunder-deafened hearing, and sending his perception out as far as the elements would allow. Surges of power came from the shoreline behind him, rivalling the lightning bolts surrounding him once more. There were caves along the coast.

It must be Drostan!

His sole chance was to head straight for the island in front of him. A rod of lightning struck the pier on Eilean. Sparks flew as nature's pure energy illuminated the night. He was nearer to the island than he'd estimated. If only he could direct this miniscule vessel through the heaving sea. Huge killer breakers surged against the shore of the tiny island, pounding one after another. If he could ride a wave, he would reach the shore. He took a deep breath and focussed—he would chance the surf, the torrent, and the tempest.

He gritted his teeth and faced them all head-on.

Drostan floated high over the cave's pond and sensed every particle of nature's force directed against Vygeas. He drew power from the surrounding rocks, which he now used as his conduit, strengthening him. He reached his hands and spirit out and searched for yet more. It came from the walls, the roof of the cave, the rock bowl in which the pond sat, and the stalactites themselves.

Only now, when filled to overflowing, was he truly alive. This was what he lived for. He yearned for more—ached so deeply for it.

Drostan trusted the elements would bring Vygeas' death. He could leave them to their course and savour every moment of this magic force of the universe.

He sucked more energy from every source available to him. It came from the earth, deep in the centre of this world's core, the derivation of all beginnings, the foundation of all. It flowed to the surface, through bedrock and shale, focused on this shoreline cave—and him.

Below Drostan, in the natural divination bowl, a wave surged. It picked up momentum and the seabed's contents then roared toward Vygeas.

"Aye! Go my friend. Kill my foe."

The one who removed from me the chance of love.

And oh, how he longed for it for many an aching year and filled his empty heart with magic's power—*the only equal consolation.*

He dragged vital force from the very base rock on which the cave and land sat. He drew in more, his source now filling him, pushing self-control far away. Like a drunkard, he staggered through his inebriated thoughts, his soul intoxicated. Sharp power burned through him as a lightning bolt, coursed through his spirit, into his soul and seared his mind.

Torched by its burn he tried to pull back, but like an enslaved intoxicant, he could not. Overcome, his soul now lost to the mastery of his addiction.

A surge of energy hit Vygeas. It came from the shoreline where he sensed Drostan. Vygeas spun as a wall of grey water rose behind him. It swirled with light brown sand, three times his height at least. He dug with his cupped hands over the side of the boat and sought to direct the point of his prow toward Eilean. The wave struck him and lifted the boat up, carried him among the churning sands and water, heading him to the island. The gathering wave sucked back water from the shore of the island of Eilean and rocks reared up ahead. On the crest of the wave Vygeas headed right for them.

"Blades and—!" His voice drowned in the surging water that carried him headlong to the rocks. They would smash his body and take his life—and any chance he had left with Leynarve.

A thunderclap numbed his ears, rumbling through him and shaking his very soul.

Then silence.

The rain stopped and the wind died down. The wave's surge lost momentum, the last of its energy driving his boat directly to the rocks. Wood cracked and splintered. The force of the blow tossed Vygeas out and dragged his limbs behind him like a rag doll. His back thrust hard against broken planks and his sword's firm length dug into his back. Cold engulfed him and waves pushed him against the rocks, their solidity startling him into action. He grasped a boulder, held tight till the surge of sand-swirled wave receded.

He dragged himself forward with burning arm muscles, hooked his heel and kicked himself up onto the flat surface of the rock, away from the swiftly dying waves, taking breaths of cool night air.

Spray from another breaker showered him with saltwater, drenching him further.

"Och, what's a wee bit more?" he said to the sky. He stood, wet clothes dragging, and trudged to the shoreline. He fell to the ground and rolled onto his back, heaving for air, senses brine-saturated.

The stars were out.

The wind had died and left a silent sky. Once roiling clouds were now still, grey shadows travelling gently past the night's starry host. The waves, which moments earlier had been roaring sea dragons, were now the soft lap of calm.

Vygeas reached out and sought Drostan. The mage's power had surged with the storm's crescendo, mirrored each lightning's flash, then dissolved with the abating winds and diminishing cloud.

Nothing.

The shore on the mainland was devoid of any trace of the mage.

His breathing settled and legs ceased their shaking, so he rolled over and stood, bracing himself against the rocky cliff-face. He stepped gingerly, his grey coat weighing down his shoulders, sodden material wrapping around his legs, impeding his stride.

He flung it off, dropping it onto the sand like slops from a bucket, and staggered on.

Another storm began—this one was in his heart.

Its thunder rang with Leynarve's voice.

Do you still intend to kill Gille Fhialain?

FIFTEEN

THE MAGE'S SANCTUARY

Bram placed the fresh-picked herbs on the long bench in his master's work-shop, the cool, still moist leaves soft beneath his fingertips. The scent of rosemary and lavender, overpowering yarrow and plantain, permeated the room.

Two days had passed without communication from Drostan.

Bram held his shoulders tight, and his stomach burned acidic, something he had not experienced since leaving his homeland and kin, and travelling across what seemed like the world, to the island of Innesfarne to study under the master mages. And now he must find how his own master fared. He would try to not disturb his activities but seek his location and observe.

Bram slid the bolt further along the door's lock, ensuring none could enter his master's chamber where the stone-carved divination bowl resided. Bram trusted the *staying* he placed on the door's bolt to hold.

I will have no intrusions from that impatient man they called lord.

The man was too bold and discourteous, held no respect for the magic arts, and treated Drostan like a servant.

"Does he know not the power the sorcerer wields?" Bram's deep voice echoed in the quiet chamber.

No, Lord Ciarán did not.

Bram paused with the acknowledgement.

He stood by the dish, its surface as still as a loch on a tranquil day, and just as reflective. The image in his mind of his home in the high mountains of Dál Gaedhle brought a tightness to his throat. He swallowed it away. No time for sentimentality. Drostan, his master and teacher, had not yet reported in and once again the day grew late.

Bram stilled his body, set aside all reminiscences of home, calmed his mind, and directed his inner vision onto the bowl.

Sensing a churning disruption, he opened his eyes to a troubled, roiling surface where once was a glassy sheen. He placed his hands on either side of the dish to steady himself and see with clarity. Stone as cold as the deep ground cooled his palms resting on the rim. He slid his hands into the water and willed his soul to dive in.

His true self flew through the darkening night, beneath thunderous clouds and over rain lashed fields, skirting wave dashed shore and broad pebbled beach. Bram dived to the ground and, drawn by the emission of power, slid through a slit in rock.

He entered a cave, a roar filling the confined space now surrounding him in rock. A sharp shining stalactite dropped from the ceiling into the roiling, boiling waters of a massive subterranean pond directly beneath. The spray flew through Bram's spirit leaving an impression of heavy minerals.

A plexus of energy drew Bram's soul and he turned to where it focused on a dark-robed form. Two sandaled feet extended from an outcropping of rock now washed by waves from the miniature ocean crashing over the side of the subterranean pool.

Bram drew closer, following the line of the legs of the person so familiar.

It *was* his master's form.

Drostan lay behind a natural lectern where no doubt he had orated his spell, the effects of this still energising the cave around him but seeming to decline by the moment.

He called to Drostan, his spirit reaching out.

Drostan moved not.

Bram drew even closer. If only he could reach out a give a physical touch! Shake Drostan's shoulder. Roll him over to look him in the eye.

But not a movement. Not a breath. Not a stirring of life.

No sense of his master's soul emanated from his inert body.

No! Drostan, my tutor and mentor, is gone.

Empty ache threatened to overtake him, overwhelm him, and strengthen any desire to return to his own body by the divination bowl

But I will stay here! There was more he must discover.

If he was in his physical form, he would gather the man in his arms. Tell him he admired him above all others. Then the last words Drostan heard would be Bram's own, promising to carry on the work where he had left off.

Traces of power filled the cave even as the storm in the miniature sea abated, the energy drawing away from Drostan's body.

Bram hovered over his master. It was like he slept, such as the times when sedated for days after using his magic, as if passed out with too much herb, leaving Bram to attend his master's chores himself. Bram shook his head as other instances of Drostan's over imbibing had left the sorcerer invigorated and Bram would run to keep up with him.

But his master's inert body told a more serious tale.

Drostan has taken in too much power.

The mages of Innesfarne warned against too much magic. They usedthe word *addiction*. It clasped on to a mage tighter and tighter if imbibed too often. *You must master the power*, they said. *Or it would master you*.

Drostan now lay stilled, evidence of the truth his mage instructors espoused.

Bram sighed and gazed at his mentor's lifeless form and pushed away what he would feel.

He would not give in to these emotions until his soul re-joined his body. Then and only then would he allow the ache to fill him and spill from his eyes in his body's own salt water.

The energy had hovered in the far corner of the cave and now surged, directed at him.

It was familiar...not Drostan. But an essence *in* his master. He had sensed it when they met in that space *in between*.

Bram held his soul tight, straining to discern the source of this living power. It filled the cave, yet it focused on the body of his tutor. Bram hovered over the black-robed form as the torch's glow dimmed by the moment, yet the intense spiritual sensation that surrounded him increased.

The eyeless sentient energy inspected Bram then beckoned him. Bram's spirit tingled with recognition of its call, his master's source now offering itself to him. He moved closer and stretched out his soul to embrace it. The power flew to him, shuddering him as the primordial force filled his soul and his world.

Now this his very existence—all else an insignificant, bland, soundless blur.

Bram awoke in his body. The hard wooden floor seeped cool into his cheek, and his arms folded in an embrace of the pedestal holding the stone divination bowl. An owl's call flitted through the narrow window of the tower chamber. The pale light of a half-moon shone, casting its gleam into his eyes. He blinked and let go of the pedestal, patted his coarse robe, rubbed his stubbled chin, and ran his fingers through his long hair.

He was the same, but not. In his inner being he was anew.

I have my master's power.

And must do my master's work.

Sixteen

The Isle of Eilean

Vygeas' boots squelched with every tread and his clothing clung to him as he lugged his feet one after the other. Cold touched his bones. The bandage on his shoulder sat above the collar of his sodden leather armour, the blood-soaked material chafing his neck.

Directly ahead lay the market square. It was peaceful now, with barrows tidied away, goods packed, covered, and locked for the night. Two streets were before him. On his left was a row of dwellings. The main cobbled road stretched ahead and led to the caisteal bailey at the peak of the mount of this small island. Larger buildings lay to his right, possibly the workrooms and storehouses belonging to the many merchants who resided and traded on this diminutive piece of land. He may find the trade and merchandising premises with Gille Fhialain's own weaving enterprise among them. The scroll Lord Ciarán had allowed him to glimpse showed a warehouse belonging to the merchant near the wharf on the far side of the island.

Clank-clacking came from far down this street to his right. Each building had a sign hanging out front. Five signs along, a picture of a loom swung on its hinges and shadows flittered across the light cast on the cobbles outside a workroom window. Perhaps Gille Fhialain's labourers and weavers were still hard at work.

Vygeas stood taller and strode to the light and sound. Voices flowed from within along with the odour of emotions.

Anxiety's shimmer. Desperation's thrum. Hunger's acid stench.

Aye, Gille Fhialain's enterprise for certain.

He knocked on the door and the voices ceased.

"Hello." Vygeas pounded on the door. "I wish to speak to the one in charge."

The hiss of voices *shushing* came from inside the building. The curiosity of the occupants headed his way, a deep purple seeping out the crack between wood and the stone threshold, then the door flew open.

"Who are you?" A tall man with hunched shoulders and a hooked nose peered at him defensively with beady eyes.

"I am a brother. Please, may I come in? I wish to speak with you."

The small dark eyes raked down his long form and up again, pausing on the dagger on his belt and the sword handle sitting high above his shoulder.

"Believe me, I am a friend." Vygeas held up his raw knuckled hands.

The man hesitated, then stepped aside to reveal a room of men, women, and children. Some sat behind the wooden frames of looms which now had ceased their *clank-clunk*. The bright-coloured cloth of a superior quality stretched flat before them as it lay tautly tied to the looms. Other workers stood and wound spools of thread. A soft fluff floated through the air.

A woman coughed and rose from a loom. More coughing came from workers in the back of the room. Bolts of fine-quality cloth sat in rows along the side wall and three men loaded more bolts into crates. None of those present wore clothing made of cloth resembling any of that on the bolts. The people were thin and dark shadows sat below their eyes. Everyone ceased their work and stared at Vygeas.

The man who had opened the door slammed it behind him and stepped up to Vygeas.

"You're an assassin, aren't you? I *knew* it!" His eyes lit up with glee and he emanated the golden mist of excitement and justification.

"What do you know?" Vygeas cut through the wary enthusiasm in the room, as thick as mustard's sharp cloy.

No one answered. Eyes found the floor more interesting. Chagrin now fogged the room.

"Who is your master?"

"Gille Fhialain, lord," Beady-eyes answered.

"And who are you?"

"I'm Arthur and I'm in charge here. Who might *you* be, lord?"

"I'm Vygeas. I wish to help you."

Around the room, workers' eyes widened. A man near Arthur placed his hand over his mouth and coughed, stepping beside him. "Ask what he wants. Make certain he's an assassin," he whispered to Arthur.

"I *am* an assassin," Vygeas admitted.

The scent of pleased-shock, the aroma like over-ripe summer fruit, rippled through the room, yet fear lingered in the corners.

"I know your merchant lord has been mistreating you. That he has not paid you for many months and your families cry in hunger while your lord and master grows fat."

"Are ye going to rid us of him?" the man next to Arthur asked.

A *shush* came from many lips and echoed around the room. Uncomfortable glances darted at Vygeas.

"I am sure to not be the only visitor to this island who chooses to earn his living by"—Vygeas tilted his head— "dealing with your problem."

Arthur double blinked. Surprise and alarm wafted from the labourers who surrounded Vygeas, the whites of their eyes glinting in the candlelit room.

"It pleases some of you," Vygeas stated. "The prospect of the man who oppresses you being...dispensed with. But I tell you, you will never receive that which is owed to you if he is. Nor will ye be able to live with yourselves if success occurs this night." Vygeas cast his gaze around the room at the group pondering his words.

"He has wealth,"—an older woman at a loom shouted— "and we can help ourselves to it when he's gone."

"And fight your way past the assassin who kills him and thinks *they* have the right to it?" Vygeas shook his head. "I don't think the odds are for you."

"What are you proposing?" Arthur asked. "For ye ken oor master leaves on the very next tide to gather his raw materials. Gold thread, raw silk, and such that can only be bought on other shores."

Och! I only have this very night to complete my task!

"Tell me all you know about where he keeps his money and hidden wealth, and I will endeavour to *obtain* it for you all when I have ...concluded my contract."

"Ye would do that?" Arthur's eyebrows rose above his beady eyes. "It is a rarity that a fellow such as yourself would suggest a scheme to folk like us. Neither would he carry it through."

"Aye, my lord will pay me once I have completed business with your lord," Vygeas responded. "I promise you. You will receive your wages."

"Promise?" A heavy hint of mistrust permeated this comment from the man beside Arthur, its stench hitting his nostrils.

"I give my word." Vygeas spoke low and firm.

"And how does this benefit ye?" Arthur asked. "Why would ye do that for us, lord assassin?"

All eyes looked Vygeas' way. Disbelief and scepticism came at him in droves, and he planted his feet, then paused.

Why am *I offering my services with the prospect of no financial return?*

The answer struck him as hard as the thunderclaps in that storm—thudding to his core.

"My redemption." He stood taller in the silent room. "I need...freedom from my past deeds." He gripped his dagger hilt as he spoke his convictions to complete strangers.

Or was the saying of it giving truth to the thoughts he'd so long pushed aside?

Aye, Leynarve was right. He had found his enemy within. It had stopped him in his tracks, and he needed to deal with his past.

Now.

A woman with salt and pepper-grey hair and wearing a threadbare skirt, stepped up to him.

"Ye are bleeding, assassin. Let us tend to your wounds afore ye go do yer work."

"I agree not with your task, my lord assassin." The older woman whispered as she re-dressed his shoulder wound. "I cannae be your conscience, young man, and I know not the past deeds from which you seek guilt-freedom. Nor do I wish to contemplate them." She secured the bandage. "But mind your choices this night. Your present, your past, and your future are bound as tightly as the Endless Knot itself."

Vygeas flinched at the older woman's words. They were the words of a sage. He held her stare, her eyes as grey as her hair. "Were you once a sage—?"

The woman's hand flew to his lips and prevented any further questions, then she removed it and pointed to the clean, neat dressing to his shoulder.

"Thank you." Vygeas tried to brush aside her curious remark.

He passed through the crowd of workers to the front door. Shame and discomfort seeped out from a few—at the prospect of their employer's death, no doubt. At least some possessed a conscience not beaten down by mistreatment.

The older woman with the healing skills and wise words walked up to him holding out half a loaf of bread, generosity filling her expression.

Vygeas shook his head. "Thank you, but no. How can I eat when ye are hungry?" He gently pushed the loaf back to the woman's chest. "Feed yourselves."

The woman clutched the loaf to herself and smiled.

Vygeas walked to the front door of the workshop, opened it a crack and cast his senses over the town. Stirrings of emotion and activity came to him. The near slumberous thoughts of Eilean's inhabitants bedding down for the night mixed with the alertness and vigilant observations from his competitors. Someone tugged his arm.

"For you, lord assassin." Arthur held a folded grey garment. "Ye are coatless, and your armour is not enough cloaking in the night."

Vygeas took the garment from him and held it up. A long, hooded coat of fine wool-thread in a deep-grey, unfolded before him. Vygeas swallowed.

"This is a gift I will accept. I thank you all." He bowed to the workers gathered behind Arthur.

Vygeas dressed in the coat, strapped his sword over his shoulder and left. He snuck to the side of the village where the dwellings sat. A moon in its last quarter, shining a weak light on Eilean, had risen late. Arthur had described his master's house. Last on the hill of finer houses, a thatched roof, white-washed stone and mortar, abutting the caisteal outer bailey wall.

Vygeas walked with a light tread, keeping close to the fronts of houses that lined the narrow, cobbled street. It neared midnight, but many others were about—concealed in the shadows. Soft shufflings hid around every corner. Breaths stirring the night air came from the rooftops. Aromas wafted past him. Questions asked. Anticipations proffered. Calculations made. Strategies created. He was not the only *murtair* considering Fhialain this night.

Ushered on by the subterfuge of his rivals, Vygeas hastened to Gille Fhialain's front door and knocked. Heavy foot treads padded down the stair to the dark solid door, every second step creaking. A plump man in his forties stood in the open doorway wearing a nightgown and his night-cap askew, with a silver candlestick in hand. The candle's flame flickered in the night breeze coming through the doorway.

"Aye?"

Vygeas strode in, his presence the impetus for the man's backward steps. He placed a finger to his lips and pushed the door shut behind him. Moonlight sifted through stained-glass windows and reflected off heavily carved dark-wood furniture, on which fine bone china ornaments and crystal vessels sat on display. A trunk, lid open revealing folded garments within, sat in the front room.

"Gille Fhialain?"

"Aye! But who are you, who burst into my home at *this* hour? The servants dismissed and we are a-bed!" He raised his eyes to the top of Vygeas shoulder and gasped at the handle of the steel blade. "What do you want?"

"Upstairs!" Vygeas nudged the podgy belly.

The shorter man, golden curls dangling from underneath his cap, stumbled back to the carpeted stairs. Candlelight flickered and provided ghoulish shadows for their ascent.

"What is it my love—?" A woman, whose long red tresses cascaded over her shoulder and fell down her white embroidered nightgown, stood in the middle of the thick rug on the floor of the bedchamber to which Fhialain had hastened. A polished bronze mirror dully reflected moonlight into this dimly lit room.

"I know not, my dear. This man is yet to make his intentions clear." Fhialain stood in front of his wife and nudged her behind his back.

The padding of small footsteps travelled from the next room and approached the chamber.

Arrow heads and fletching! Fhialain could have a quiver full of children. Leynarve had said he had family, but not how many.

A spike of the acrid scent of fear mingled with curiosity's spice floated ahead of two young girls pushing past him to their parents. Curls bounced and long night gowns fluttered.

Only two.

"No, darlings! Stay back!" Fhialain shouted at his daughters.

"Too late, my love." Hardness edged Fhialain's wife's voice. "He's seen them."

Fear's sharp odour peaked from the parents as their daughters ran closer and hugged them.

In front of the four-poster bed, hung with silk curtaining and heavy damask drapes, the family clung to each other and stared at Vygeas. His hooded coat and broadsword, and the dagger at his belt would make his intentions obvious to them all.

Vygeas ground his teeth. He'd been here before. Children were *never* on his list. His plan of a direct approach and sensible conversation with Fhialain would not work. He flicked his fingers, dancing them against his thigh. He had modified his methods because of the competition waiting outside.

Plus Leynarve's words.

Aye. They have worked on me.

But now here he was—Fhialain's beautiful wife and two gorgeous daughters in the mix. Blast that Lord Ciarán! The *game* would entangle these three innocents in its trap and the other assassins out there may not believe as he did.

Fhialain and his family's lives were now forfeit.

The whimpers of the folk in front of him, combined with the tapping of his dancing fingers on his leather breeches, provided an accompaniment to the montage before him. Vygeas chewed the scar on the corner of his mouth. It was thick and tugged to annoyance.

Time to decide, Vygeas. Remember redemption?

"Why haven't you paid your labourers?" Vygeas growled.

Fhialain's wife sucked in her breath and hushed her startled girls, and Fhialain lifted his chin.

"I...ah..." Fhialain began.

"You are a greedy, selfish man. You live in this mansion while your workers starve. I have just met with them. Some are not well and cannot afford a healer sage."

"They put you up to this?" Incredulity tinged the merchant's tone. Outrage flowed from him.

"Oh, no." Vygeas laughed. "Your greed has won you notoriety. I'm not the only one after you this night."

"Oh, Mama." The oldest of the little girls grabbed tighter to her mother's nightgown. The stench of fear emanated from all four.

Vygeas' heart pounded within him as his throat threatened to close tight.

He would not kill this family. He would *not* complete this job and leave more victims.

"This is what will happen." Vygeas' voice rang loud in the now quiet room.

SEVENTEEN

THE FOREST BY THE SHORELINE

Dräger's uncomfortable whinnies died down with the wind. The storm ceased as quickly as it had begun, and the stallion calmed his tense prancing while the roaring in the treetops settled.

Leyna released the clench on her lower lip and swallowed. "V would have been out in that."

"Aye, my lady." Aiden nodded, his mouth a thin line.

A tightness gripped Leyna's throat as she ran her hands through her curls. Had he survived? She shook herself. She was still angry with him! Vygeas—the very object of her desire for revenge that had simmered over these past five years.

What of *that* now? Her hand stilled in her hair, entangled by knot-filled curls and her purposeful march to the Isle of Eilean stopped in its tracks. The assassin found. Was she now concerned for his welfare? She grunted a laugh, a confused noise even to her own hearing.

What of retribution? What of justice and punishment? She grit her teeth, growling at the place where vengeance sat.

"My lady?" Aiden bent his head to her face.

She blinked the lad's visage away from her focus. Did V deserve punishment ... or was he just the weapon in Lord Ciarán's hands? Aye, perhaps Ciarán Gallawain was the true murderer on that account.

The tightness in that place between her shoulders eased.

But what of the assassin now? Perhaps he survived that storm and now goes to complete his task.

"Only one way to know for certain." Leyna grabbed Dräger's reins from Aiden.

"My lady, I'll come with you."

"No, you stay here. I may not like what I find." She swallowed hard. Vygeas death in this storm would be justice, would it not? A rare occasion when fate intervened. Her parents' assassin dealt with by nature's force. So why was it difficult to stop the ache that arose?

"No, my lady," Aiden said. "Begging your pardon. My Lord Vygeas ordered me to protect you. I will accompany you." His brow creased in the middle.

He was still on about that? Aiden had never been so intense.

"I wish to know the fate of my lord, my Lady Leyna." He glanced at his feet.

"Very well." Leyna placed her knee in Aiden's interlaced hands then he boosted her into the saddle of the tall horse. She assisted him to mount behind her.

Leyna kicked the war horse to a gallop and headed for the village looking out over to Eilean. She came upon fallen trees strewn along the main road to the village and, pulling Dräger to a walk, picked her way around branches and thicker tree trunks. Loose leaves flitted across the road and in between the war horse's hooves. The scent of singed wood and settling leaf litter hit her nostrils, gaining in intensity as they neared the hamlet by the pier.

The power of the passing storm had cleaved the pier in two. It smoked as sailors and villagers alike doused it with buckets of water. Boats of all sizes, now loosed from their moorings, lay strewn throughout the bay. A few had run aground on the shoreline itself. Over by Eilean, the debris of a boat gathered on the rocky shore. No bodies lay in Leyna's view.

"I must know for certain." She dismounted and threw Aiden the reins "Hold Dräger."

Leyna walked along the slatted pier to where it smouldered. There was a gap the size of a small dwelling before the pier slats resumed and smoke rose from the closest boards.

"Excuse me, sir," she said to the back of a grey-haired, solidly built man.

The boatman paused in his dousing of the pier slats and turned an irritated stare to her.

"What do ye want? I'm a wee bit busy at present."

"If you please, can you tell me if a man with a sword travelled across in a boat about the time of the storm just passed?"

"Oh." The man rubbed the back of his neck with a solid weather-beaten hand. "Do ye see the broken planks on the other shore there, lass?" His tone now softer as he pointed.

Leyna scanned the smashed wood by the rocks on the far shore of Eilean and swallowed. "Aye." She couldn't keep the forlorn note from her voice.

"Well, I dinnae ken if that's the man ye are looking for, but that's ma boat I hired to a tall man in a grey cloak and a broadsword as big as ye are, lass. Sorry, but I dinnae ken where he is the noo'."

No. Leyna's heart seemed to miss a beat as it sank into her belly. She spun and ran back to Aiden.

"That was the boat." Leyna flung her arm behind her and pointed at the wreck. "But I need to know for sure. I'll row over, you stay here."

"No, my lady, I'll not hold the horse and desert my lord. I'm coming."

"But what about Dräger?"

"My lord gave me coin. I'll hire someone to mind him." Aiden's intense blue eyes stopped any protest forming in her throat.

"Very well, but it won't be safe there, Aiden—"

"I ken." He had dismounted and now led the stallion to the nearest dwelling. "I must sharpen your short-sword, my lady. My Lord Vygeas gave me a dagger. We must be well armed."

"So, you now forgive him, my lady?" Aiden manned the oars as Leyna peered ahead through the light of the quarter moon, her vision fixed on the boat wreckage, a dark shadow on the moonlit shoreline of Eilean.

Hiring a boat had not been easy for many were now possessive of their craft that had survived the storm. Gold convinced them.

"No." Leyna's voice was firm. "I only want to know if he survived."

"And what then, my lady?"

Leyna did not answer. Aiden's story of throwing away grievance to the winds rang in her head. She had worn her need for vengeance like an old familiar garment for so long. She huffed. It was said that one's clothing makes the person what they are. Did she want revenge to consume her? Maybe her desire to kill the assassin who executed her parents would destroy her as the young knave had declared. But now it was clear Lord Ciarán was the real guilty one. But Vygeas had still played his part...

"But if ye had nae forgiven him, then ye would nae care what happened to him." Aiden startled her out of her thoughts. "Isn't that so, my lady?"

"Aiden." Leyna flicked her mind from her contemplations and bore a glassy stare into the lad. "Vygeas killed my parents. I can't just forgive him like that!" She snapped her fingers.

Aiden clamped his mouth shut and rowed on.

They reached the shoreline of the island and Aiden ran the boat into the sand, jumped out, and pulled it further up the narrow beach. Leyna hopped out and helped him drag it near the rocks strewn with wreckage of the shattered boat.

No sign of a human, alive or dead. An invisible hand clamped around her rib cage. She ran up to the rocks with Aiden and searched.

Nothing. The hand tightened its grip, now squeezing her stomach.

"My lady?" Hope laced Aiden's voice as he pointed to the strip of dry sand leading to the cobblestone ramp that made its way through the gates. Footprints began here and ended at the walkway. Large footprints.

"It could be anyone." Leyna swallowed; her throat seemed lined with sand.

Aiden walked further on while she stared at the huge boot imprint, the sand in her throat washing away.

"My lady!" Aiden's eyes lit up as he first pointed and then dragged something from beside the city gate. He held a shredded, grey, soaked garment. "It's my lord's. He must have made it, my lady! He's here on Eilean."

Leyna closed her eyes and sighed. He'd survived the wreck. Vygeas was alive. But that meant he would attend to his mission. Her eyes flew open.

And kill again.

The moonlight glowed off the city's honey-coloured sandstone walls.

"Come. We've got to get to him. Try to stop him."

"Stop him, my lady? But then Lord Ciarán will hang him—!"

"If Vygeas wants my pardon, he needs to show me he's a changed man." Leyna faced Aiden full on, her words sharp. "Does he not?"

Aiden blinked. "Aye, my lady but—"

"But what?"

"Forgiveness depends not on the one to be forgiven, but the one doing the forgiving. If ye don't mind me correcting ye, my lady." Aiden bobbed his head.

Leyna raised her eyebrows, mulling over his comments. *Oh, I don't have time for this!*

"Come!" She dragged Aiden by the arm and through the gates. "And be quiet."

One side of the square led off to workshops, the other, to dwellings. She turned that way.

Leyna examined the street. A long row of wealthy houses lined it, most double storey, the roofs were slate or thatch. Slate was convenient—easy to climb and the best way to see any town was from a high vantage point.

"Follow me." Leyna chose a house with a frontage of dark wood which framed white-washed stone in square sections up the walls. The timber jutted outwards just enough for a toe-grip or handhold. A climbing rose wound itself through a trellis that reached the second floor. Hand over hand Leyna climbed.

"My lady?" Aiden's voice choked.

"Shh! Come on, you can do it." She picked the way up the house wall and settled on the slanting roof. Aiden had made it to the second floor and clutched onto a window frame. He looked up, his expression a cross between fear and triumph. Leyna undid her sword belt, her short sword still in its scabbard, and held it down to him. Aiden grasped it and she pulled him up, guiding his climb as he navigated to the roof. Beaming, he crawled and sat beside her.

She led the way across rooftops in a crouch, and along to the rear where most dwellings stopped shy of the outer bailey wall of the caisteal. From the corner of her vision, she caught movement ahead. Far ahead along the outer bailey wall, a large man in a hooded dark-grey coat climbed out of the window of a thatched house. He squatted on the wall as he assisted a woman in trousers, two young children and a rotund man, out of a window. They carried bundles and bags, making their progress cumbersome.

It was Vygeas. Those broad shoulders were his, *and* that stubbled chin sticking out of the hood.

Behind her, Aiden took in air as if to speak. Leyna spun and covered his mouth with her hand. Vygeas was up to something. But what was it? Her brow cooled with a sheen of sweat. He could be carrying out his mission on this family. What would he say if he knew she was here?

Vygeas and his companions edged their course along the wall toward the double tower gate of the caisteal. Leyna stayed put until he was almost out of sight and out of hearing. She twisted back to Aiden, her hand still on his mouth.

"That's your lord," she whispered. "We must follow but at such a distance he won't sense us." Leyna screwed her face in a grimace. "However far that may be," she continued her whisper with her hand over Aiden's mouth. "We must be silent as we tail him. Do you understand?" She kept her glare on him.

Aiden nodded, her hand clasped to his mouth moving up and down, his bright blue eyes never leaving hers. Leyna took her hand away and pointed in the direction in which Vygeas had gone. They stepped with care along the narrow top of the wall of the outer bailey, for being far from the double tower gate, it had no walkway attached.

There was movement on a roof further ahead. Leyna stopped and leaned back onto the top storey wall of the next dwelling. She pulled Aiden with her and squeezed him into a niche in the stonework. A caped and hooded figure with a criss-cross of swords on his back, jumped soundlessly from the roof ahead and walked toe-to-toe along the wall after Vygeas and his group.

Leyna's heart rate spiked. Vygeas wasn't the only one who knew Fhialain was the mark, and going by the weather, autumn's winds would be severe this season, and if Fhialain had any sense, he would sail as soon as possible. Tonight may be anyone's last chance. As per Lord Ciarán's plan, other assassins were pursuing the merchant. That would make Vygeas' job more difficult.

Oh. Leyna let out a long, quiet breath. Lord Ciarán's game had been with Vygeas, and him alone. That horrible lord had sent Vygeas on a mission almost impossible to complete. Playing with the man's hope of escaping the hangman's noose and obtaining his freedom. Leyna stifled a growl at Lord Ciarán's cruelty. She gasped at her thoughts, stumbled through them. Her caring for Vygeas slapped at her.

She did not want this man dead—no matter what he had done to her past.

Leyna placed her finger to her lips, indicating to Aiden to continue his silence, then stepped behind this assassin. Aiden followed, balancing along the top of the wall.

Vygeas and his company had reached the caisteal gate tower in the outer bailey wall and now negotiated with the guards. Vygeas' deep voice carried to Leyna through the cool night air. The quarter-moon shone on both Vygeas and the assassin who followed, glinting on the assassin's swords. He drew closer to the gate tower, slowly removing the blades from their scabbards.

Leyna's pulse thudded in her ears, and she quickened her pace. She must be as silent as night itself. Approaching the assassin, she drew her short sword. The assassin faced Vygeas' conversation in the tower, listening ahead. Leyna tightened her grip on her weapon and thrust it up and into the assassins' side, her razor-sharp blade sliding between ribs. A rasping sound came from the man before her as air sucked through the wound in his chest. He twisted and looked at her, losing balance and falling into the courtyard below. Frothy blood came from his mouth opening wide, like his eyes.

Leyna retreated to the nearest dwelling and pressed her back against its roof, out of sight as a dull thud echoed below the wall. Aiden was beside her.

The conversation with the guards at the gate tower paused for a moment, then footsteps descended the stairs and out the gate.

EIGHTEEN

THE WAREHOUSE

Leyna leaned into the wall, and ensured Aiden did the same, as Vygeas and his party's muffled footsteps headed away from the gate tower of the inner bailey wall. Leyna silently counted to ten, then beckoned for Aiden to follow and with soft steps walked along the top of the wall. Right before the gate tower, where no structures abutted the wall, she squatted and turned to Aiden.

Leyna pointed to herself and then to the ground below and mouthed, 'You follow me.'

Aiden raised his brow and his shoulders, opening his mouth as if about to speak. She clamped her hand over his lips and shook her head. He halted his speech and nodded, her hand performing its same comical dance with his face. When she was sure of his silence, she let go. Leyna turned and with her face toward the wall, eased herself down. She held on and dangled her legs, smiling encouragement to Aiden. Leyna let her arms extend and dropped her body to the ground.

Aiden's head peeped over the top of the wall directly above her, his curls covered his eyes, but his mouth gaped open. She wriggled her fingers in a *come-down* gesture. He shook his head. She placed her hands on her hips. The corners of his mouth curled downward.

Leyna held her palms outward and raised her eyebrows. She pointed firmly to herself. 'I'm going,' she mouthed and turned to the street heading for the other side of the steep hill and the caisteal complex.

Feet thudded at the base of the bailey wall. "Psst!" Aiden stepped in and followed her.

They sidled along together, hugging close to walls, and crested the mount. Below sat many long-roofed buildings—warehouses. A cluster of smaller buildings by the wharves stood even further below on the other side of this mount. Ships docked by the wharf in readiness to sail at the next high tide, their canvas sails reflecting the faint moonlight, tightly bound, ready for the dawn wind to unfurl and fill them.

A group of figures approached the warehouses. Wrapped in cloaks, two young girls and a woman lugged their belongings. Vygeas' tall form followed them while the plump man led the way. There was a clatter and a spark off the cobblestones near Vygeas' feet, skidding behind him and barely missing the children. He pushed his companions onward to the nearest warehouse.

"What was that?" Aiden broke his silence.

Leyna resisted the urge to spin on Aiden and clasp her hand firmly over his open mouth. She viewed the buildings opposite the warehouse and followed the imagined trajectory of the arrow back to its source. Nothing. Leyna slid her gaze back to Vygeas. He turned and for a fraction of time looked up in the same direction. An arrow *thunked* beside him, its iron tip embedded in the warehouse's doorframe at head-height. Vygeas ducked through the door and out of sight of his would-be assassin, the door banging shut behind him.

"They could corner him." Leyna turned to Aiden. "Watch where Vygeas goes next." Her whisper was harsh. "He won't use this exit. Move over that way,"— Leyna pointed to the other end of the building— "and see if he comes out there."

Aiden crept in the direction Leyna had indicated then she slid through the shadows to the source of the arrows. She scanned the rooftops, keeping one ear on the door Vygeas had just entered.

Would Vygeas slaughter the family in there?

A shadow straightened on the parapet of the rooftop directly opposite the door of the warehouse—a female figure silhouetted by the night, her hair flowing behind with the breeze. She had a longbow in her hand and a quiver hung from her waist. Leyna scoured the building the woman stood upon. An alleyway ran beside it. A narrow stairway on the side of the building led up to the roof. Leyna ascended, placing each foot with care as she leaned down and retrieved her thin throwing knives from her right boot.

She reached the top in silence. Her target still faced the warehouse. Leyna took a breath and held one of her throwing knives in a relaxed grip. She calculated she was six feet away from this woman. That was two rotations of her six-inch blades. Leyna aimed and threw. It landed short and clattered on the slate roof.

Dragon's teeth!

The archer turned, notching an arrow. Leyna stepped forward and threw again, two in quick succession. Her revised calculations should hit their mark. An arrow flew. Leyna twisted to the side with her last throw as the *whirr* of the shaft and fletching passed her face.

All my knives gone. She grasped her bloodied short sword.

The assassin on the roof's edge stood motionless, looking down at her front, and dropping her bow. The arrow from her other hand joined its clatter on the rooftop. The woman faced Leyna and held her gaze as she toppled back, her falling arched silhouette revealing two knife handles protruding from her chest. A dull thud echoed up from the ground.

Leyna's mouth went dry.

What have I done? Two lives taken in such a short space of time. She had been a thief. She was now a murderer. How simple it had been. But she'd protected Vygeas, and she would do so again. She crawled to retrieve her knife from near the roof's edge, her hands shaking. Leyna wrapped her fingers around the stray throwing knife, shut her eyes, and placed her forehead on the slate roof.

Cold touched her brow, and her heart.

Aye, how easy it could be to justify an action, even one such as taking another's life. Vygeas stated he operated from this very viewpoint.

Who am I to judge another's deeds? All are capable of vile acts.

None are exempt.

Below, a door opened, and footsteps made their way past the building.

"What are you doing here?" Vygeas' whisper echoed up from the small alley beneath her.

Nineteen

Restitution

"My lord?" Aiden choked.

"Where's Lady Leynarve? Who's holding Dräger?"

"Ah—"

"Och, I dinnae have time for this!" A storm made its presence felt in Vygeas as his senses heightened their pitch. Aiden would not be here without Leynarve. Why was the lad so reticent? Astonishment sat on the roof above him and a vague hint of the scent that was Leynarve wafted over to him. Vygeas recounted his night's activity—Leynarve's perfume had been there all along. Distant and thin, her fragrance had followed him. But the lad was giving nothing away.

"You can assist me. Do ye still have that dagger I gave you?"

Aiden nodded.

"Very well. Come with me." Vygeas turned back to the warehouse where Fhialain and his family sat restrained in case of flight. He passed once again the body of a woman archer.

"What about my lady, my lord?" Anxiety came from the lad in droves, and the sweet aroma of fond concern.

"I think she can look after herself for a wee while, don't you?" Vygeas indicated with his chin to the body smashed on the cobblestones with two blade handles protruding from the ribs of the feminine torso. "She won't speak to me, will she?"

"Ah...no, my lord."

"Why did she follow me, then?"

Aiden didn't answer.

So, she still hated him. *I can find no blame in such a sentiment.*

"What's in the wee box, my lord?" Aiden pointed to the small chest Vygeas held against his side.

"Wages." Vygeas pushed open the warehouse door and Aiden followed.

Fear and apprehension, mixed with hope, filled the air with a dirty rose-pink and wafted from the far corner where the Fhialain family sat restrained and bound.

"Master and Mistress Fhialain, and young maidens Fhialain." Vygeas nodded a slight bow. "My knave will keep guard to ensure you do not decide you would be better with your own plans. A mistake I wish you not to make." He patted Aiden on the shoulder. "Aiden is armed and is under my orders to prevent any escape. Let not his youth fool you. There's a body out there, if you don't believe me." He spoke into Aiden's ear. "Don't lose one of them. I shan't be long. We must get them aboard their ship before the cover of night slips away."

Aiden straightened his shoulders, a serious expression filling his face, but he emanated the strong aroma of pride and pleasure. From him it was... *oranges?*

Vygeas shrugged.

Good. Praise lavished would ensure Aiden would not fail him. Vygeas spun and strode out the door. He had wasted too much time already.

Vygeas ran his gaze along each rooftop, alleyway, and corner as he ran down the road, through the deserted market square, and back up to the workroom where Arthur would be waiting for him.

Shadows still held determined scents. Leather and chainmail creaked here and there as his fellow assassins moved through the night. A high concentration of them hovered around Gille Fhialain's home. Vygeas had removed the family in time. The guards on watch at the caisteal were alert and spiked anticipation. He picked up their distant conversation as he ran by. They had found the body of a stranger collapsed behind their walls, fully armed and foaming frothy blood from a stab wound in the side, deep between his ribs.

Leynarve remained by the warehouse, her sweet perfume receding as he moved through the town. His throat warmed.

Honed blade edge! He must stay sharp and concentrate on his task!

Vygeas approached and Arthur opened the workroom door. He was the only occupant.

Vygeas entered and held out the chest. "I have your word you will distribute it fairly?"

Arthur grasped the chest, but Vygeas retained his hold on it and leaned forward. "I'll return if I hear otherwise."

"'T will go to the needy first, my lord assassin." Arthur's beady eyes widened under his dark brows as honesty's pure aroma came from him.

"Very well. On a parchment tucked into the lid is a map to the place where your employer holds some wealth secure." Vygeas nodded and Arthur's brows reached his hairline. "I wish ye farewell and good luck with your future business venture." Vygeas turned and left, the foreman's pungent odour of surprise lingering behind him.

Vygeas smiled. The workers would do well with the merchant's trade, maybe even cause a revolution.

The night was half gone, and the rest of Vygeas' task pressed upon him. The stirrings around him had intensified. The next stage of his plan would be the most difficult. Making his way back in stealth, long learned as a necessary skill, he crossed the alleyway to the warehouse. A soft scratching on the roof opposite confirmed Leynarve's lookout post.

She had stayed out of curiosity, most likely. Vygeas sniffed, strong and deep. Leynarve's perfume retreated as he reached the door.

He entered the warehouse, low voices in amicable conversation greeted him and Aiden turned with a smile.

"Thank you, Aiden," he said. "Ye may go to the lady now. She will need you."

"But—?"

"Go."

Aiden bobbed his head.

"Farewell." Aiden smiled at the family. "I wish ye well on your journey." He waved as he left, closing the warehouse's heavy wooden door behind him with a thunk.

"What now, sir?" Fhialain asked.

"You must comply with all I command." Vygeas released Fhialain's bonds. "Do you have the bag of gold?"

"Aye, sir." Fhialain rummaged in his sac and handed Vygeas the bag.

It was heavy but small enough to tuck into his belt. Vygeas released their bonds, ordered them to stand and follow. He led the party through the far door of the warehouse, the one nearest the wharves outside.

"Quiet now." Vygeas directed his order to the children, whose fear-scent had spiked.

Moonlight reflected off the planking leading to the docked merchant ships. Water lapped with somnolence at the posts of the docks, while a gentle breeze stirred the riggings, intensifying saline impressions in Vygeas' nose. Sailors milled around in preparation for their voyages which would begin on the dawn tide. Carts loaded with provisions sat beside every second berth, where deckhands carried trunks or rolled barrels. Sailors manned the levers that lifted the nets filled with goods from the wharf and loaded them into the cargo hold of the vessel.

Vygeas paused. The sensations he had perceived from his opponents were far behind this wharf area. None had ventured any further than the archer. Providence was on the side of this family tonight.

"Which one were ye to sail on this day?" Vygeas whispered out the side of his mouth to the merchant.

"Third down. The *Dál Ghàidheal Winds*," Fhialain replied.

Vygeas led the family along and arrived at the *Dál Ghàidheal Winds*, a three master. Sailors scampered over the upper rigging and performed final checks before the grand vessel set sail.

"Who's there?" The sailor at the gangway, most likely the first mate, spoke, pausing in his directions to the deckhands.

"'Tis passengers arriving early but hoping on your kindness, sir, to let them board." Vygeas put on his most polite speech.

"Oh, aye." The first mate nodded.

Vygeas strode up the gangway, dodging a barrel, and whispered to the seaman. "We wish to speak to your captain in private."

The moon illuminated the man's weatherworn face as the first mate's eyes ran over Vygeas' sword.

"What business, like?"

Vygeas tilted his head. "One or two more passengers than expected. I'm sure your generous captain will be able to accommodate." He held up the bag of gold and gave a shake slight enough to clink the coins together. "They will settle for a simple berth."

The first mate led the way to the captain's cabin where the gold-motivated man found a larger berth for Gille Fhialain and his family and left them to settle in with their meagre belongings. The two young girls climbed into a bunk and turned to the wall, asleep in moments. Fhialain and his wife faced Vygeas.

"I never expected I would say this, but I thank you for my life, lord assassin. And I wish you well." Fhialain raised an eyebrow. "Ye gave my employees their wages?"

"Aye, merchant. Arthur will distribute them."

Fhialain snorted. "Good luck to them all."

"And now, good luck to you, sir." Vygeas withdrew his dagger from his belt. Fhialain and his wife's eyes widened, and the acrid stench of fear filled the cabin. "For my employer requires evidence that *I* have completed *my* task."

TWENTY

TIME TO LEAVE

All was quiet and still along the path from the wharf. Vygeas strained his senses. Aye, his peers gathered around the merchant's abode, now devoid of family. With luck, they would not venture afield, and the *Dál Ghàidheal Winds* would sail before the tide went out, or any assassins thought further. Vygeas leaned into a shadowed doorway, the edge of the world hinted a silver light. Sunrise was on its way to a cloudless sky.

So, Leynarve had followed him to Eilean but did not wish to speak with him. He hung his head as his fingers tapped his thigh.

She could not forgive him. Once more, he found no blame. He barely forgave himself.

For Elyse.

For Leynarve's parents.

Vygeas snorted out a breath.

"How could I ever have considered the vocation of assassin a valid one?" he muttered.

He'd reached out to Leynarve, to make reparation for his past deeds. His shoulders sank.

Without success. But he couldn't remain stuck in his tracks. He would have to do the forgiving—of himself—so he *could* move on.

"Be something better," he whispered.

Vygeas touched the small pouch at his belt, now devoid of most of its gold but containing an object of greater value—the means to his freedom from Lord Ciarán.

He would take the long route around the island to avoid assassins. He passed the tower gate and kept tight to the outer bailey wall in the opposite direction he had come with the Fhialains. He let a quiet laugh escape. The caisteal guards had accepted his story of himself as an armed escort to ensure the safety of the family and had allowed his access through the caisteal gates.

Vygeas held his senses alert. He pushed out further, seeking Leynarve and Aiden.

The hackles on his neck rose. Heated intention sped toward his back. Vygeas spun and unsheathed his weapon in one swift motion.

An Inberian warrior, wearing light mail and hooded in semi-darkness, charged at him. The assassin filled Vygeas' vision, his tungsten-alloy blade held aloft, descending to Vygeas. Vygeas stepped in, raised his broadsword, both hands firm on the grip—his body now surging with energy for the fight. Vygeas received the blow along his blade's long edge, then tilted his sword down, stabbing the warrior's neck with its point.

The man grunted and disengaged. Vygeas sliced down the man's chest, his chain maille taking most of his blow and skimming Vygeas' sword awry. The warrior let one hand go from his sword and pressed it to his neck, now spurting red. Vygeas used the momentum of his sliding blade and turned. Building energy, he followed through a complete rotation and returned to his foe with a spinning-cut aimed just above the low maille collar. The Inberian's severed head smashed to the ground, his body falling limply beside it—his disconnected hand flying wide.

Warmth splattered Vygeas cheek and more joined the sweat that moistened his brow.

He leaned against the wall, steadying himself. Clearing the battle lust.

He had to think.

So, the assassins were after *him* now.

Chills ran up his spine and competed with the white heat in his veins.

Lord Ciarán! *Drostan!*

Ghillie Fhialain was the ruse, and the bait!

Damn them!

Vygeas picked up the tungsten-alloy blade then retrieved its scabbard from the torso of his attacker. He tucked his prize into his belt and back-tracked. Vygeas ran beneath the raised portcullis, ignoring the warning calls from the guards at the tower gate. Motion came to him from all corners of Eilean. He raced to the location that was the calmest. The ancient, long narrow building with a high roof next to the caisteal keep itself—the Great Hall of Worship.

Vygeas sprinted to the double wooden doors twice his height and seized a handle. It did not budge. He beat against the doors with the pommel of his bloodied sword. The sages stirred now, early risers all.

Annoyance and surprise rose at him, from without and within. An arrow thunked into the door on the left. Followed by another as a mauve-robed sage pulled the right-hand door inward. Vygeas tore past the gasping sage.

"The way out?" Vygeas shouted at the stunned face. "Shut the door unless you want to be pierced, man!"

The sage slammed the door behind them both. Dull *thunks* came through the solid oak.

"Through to the back, my lord." The sage's speech was rapid, and he pointed to the far end of the long narrow building.

Sunlight's glow edged through the lower section of the tall windows, which were almost the full height of this grand construction. Illuminated shadows in red, purples and blues commenced their day's patchy journey within the building as the sunlight travelled through its long stained-glass windows. The ceiling was immense. Vygeas glanced up as he ran to the back of the long centre aisle. Thick brown beams spanned the width of the structure. Resting on them, V-shaped support beams kept the roof from falling on the worshippers beneath. Banners hung between the windows, suspended from the sturdy woodwork surrounding the tops of the window frames.

It had been a while since Vygeas had found himself in a place such as this. He slowed his flight.

What is it?

A long time ago he had felt *this*. It was in no building, but by a grand waterfall. Covered in its spray he had sensed the same.

Peace.

A sensation beyond description. A place where pardon was freely given, and love flowed over him.

Ripping wood screeched behind him and angry determination flooded between the fractured doors, crimson red flowing like a bloodied mist. Vygeas ran once more. A spear flew past, missing his left ear by a blade's width. He veered right.

And faced a wall. Vygeas strode ahead and grabbed the hem of the banner with a yew tree tapestried along its entire length. He grasped it and walked up the wall and lifted himself on to the wide cross beam at the top. A blond solid man in thick leather armour and two swords at his back had caught the banner in both hands and commenced walking the wall. Vygeas sliced down with his sword and cut the ropes which held the banner to the top of the wall, and it dropped. The blond assassin landed on the floor with a thud.

Vygeas cut the ties of the banner the other side of the beam and walked toe-to-toe along the cross beam. Arrows flew past him. Voices below mixed their shouts and growls—discordant noise, interrupted only by the sage's pleas for mercy. A fog of hatred and determination rose to Vygeas.

Vygeas crossed the beam to the other side and cut the ties of the nearest banner. Another assassin fell with a thud on the stone floor. Vygeas cut loose the tapestry to the right, this one empty. Drawing it up he wrapped it into a wad and wound it around his left arm. A makeshift shield. He lifted it to his face and an arrow lodged into the thickly padded folds of the heavy woven material. A spear followed it in an instant, he leaned forward, allowing it to fly past his back. He corrected his balance, held his sword tight and swatted away arrows and daggers. Surely the mêlée below would run out of weapons soon.

Further along and closer to the entrance doors, a bald assassin with a silver earring in his right ear, clambered up a remaining banner between two windows, and made for the beam above him.

Blades and bloody battle-axes. *A bloody sea-rover!* Ropes and sails were home to him and walking a beam—as simple as crawling. Vygeas braced himself on his crossbeam and took a deep breath to steady his thundering heart.

The clamour of the hall quietened. He grimaced. The rabble below would now be preparing to watch the entertainment to come on the high beams above.

TWENTY-ONE

ESCAPE

The double doors of the Great Hall of Worship burst wide. Armed guards, clad in the red caisteal precinct uniform, entered and slashed their blades through the throng of fighters below. Every head turned their way, and the clank of clashing weapons, angry shouts and curses rose to Vygeas.

Vygeas breathed hard. His glance below would cost him seconds vital in combat. He flicked his gaze across to the sea-rover where two blades spun through the air from his direction, flashes of light catching their edges. He protected his neck with the makeshift shield. Vygeas twisted side-on and a new impression of emotions welled from behind him.

A sharp thud to his shoulder muscle, followed fractions of a moment later by a piercing burn to his thigh. The sea-rover had found his mark. Vygeas steadied his balance and flicked a glance down. A blade handle protruded from his bandaged shoulder and another high on his outer thigh. He detected a familiar perfume and stood taller while a wall of rage and determination pushed from behind.

A whoosh of air passed, its origin from the rear of the building, blowing a loose strand of hair across his face.

The wash of air belonged to a throwing knife headed for the sea-rover. The eyes in the bald head opened wider. The left eye received the thin blade. It sank in deep. The man toppled, face down, and landed in the crowd of weapons and anger seething below.

Vygeas pivoted on the crossbeam, held a support-beam with his uninjured arm, and clung to his sword with the other. Leynarve stood balanced with grace on the beam farthest back, staring at him. Her sharp brown eyes darted from his shoulder to his leg. Vygeas' pulse skipped up a notch. She pointed to the wide lintel above the window frame to his left.

"Come, that way. Quickly V," she ordered.

Vygeas shook off his shield of wadded wall banner and changed his grip on the beam. Shoulder muscles stabbed by the protruding blade screamed as he held tight with that arm. He clenched his teeth against it and re-sheathed his sword with his uninjured arm, then picked his course along the crossbeam to the lintel above the nearest of the tall windows. He crept along, his boots chocked against the narrow lintels while he clutched at the crossbeams as he passed them, until he reached Leynarve deep in the back of the Great Hall of Worship.

She headed further along the beam. At this side of the building, a plain glass back window sat open.

"The way out." She faced him, triumphant.

Vygeas blinked. "Maybe for a small person but—"

"Help me push it wider, assassin. It's your only way of escape."

He leaned on the window and pushed it outward, his shoulder burning. He sucked air between his teeth. The blade handle protruding from his leg knocked the lower section of the pane. He stifled a gasp.

The window gave way and clunked open further.

"You first, V." Leynarve was urgent. "They've almost fought themselves out down there."

He levered himself up and slipped onto his back, to avoid knocking dagger handles further, and slid out onto the building below. He landed with a clank, both his sword in its scabbard across his back, and his newest acquisition tucked in his belt, hitting the slate roof.

"Whose blood is that on your face?" She landed lightly beside him and squatted.

He touched the tacky substance on his cheek. "Not mine, Leynarve."

"Those daggers will hinder us." She opened the lower part of her leather chest armour and ripped a strip of material from the hem of her blouse. Loud shouts and the clash of the mêlée within the place of worship filtered out their escape window. "This will hurt." She pulled the blade from his leg.

Searing pain spasmed his thigh. He clenched his teeth, repressing a roar.

"Give me more notice next time!" He said when he could breathe again.

She bound the oozing wound. "No major vessels, just a lot of severed muscle. You'll live from that one. Next."

"No! I'll do this one!" He covered the knife handle with his fist. "This is sore to begin with."

Leynarve curled a brow. "Not being a baby, are you?"

"No." His own defensiveness shouted at him. "Have ye got your bandage ready?"

"Aye, assassin. Ready when you are."

Vygeas wrenched the dagger from his shoulder in one brisk action and gasped for air. He laid back hard, chest heaving from pain. Shoulder on fire.

Her compassion flowed over him—a balmy aroma that warmed his soul.

She was here. Helping him. He could hope.

"We have to go," she bound his shoulder tightly. "Up, assassin!"

He rose and followed, wounds burning and torn muscles screaming. Leynarve picked her way along the narrow edges between roof tops, around corners using the lips of walls, and along their lengths until she found a place to drop. She stopped dead and flicked around a glare and, with her finger to her lips, she squatted. Vygeas crouched low, sitting beside her motionless for a time.

Below, the clatter of horses' hooves on the cobblestone road passed them. A wagon drove on the winding way to the beach—the sand causeway to the mainland when at low tide.

The day was here, but the tide was still too high to walk it. They would have to find a place to wait it out.

Vygeas gently tapped her shoulder and whispered, "I know where we can go."

TWENTY-TWO

BEGINNINGS

Vygeas pointed toward Fhialain's workshop and Leynarve picked a way along the rooftops that avoided any activity below. Vygeas pushed his perception out behind them in case of pursuit. Swirling anger and retribution remained in the Great Hall of Worship. Maybe the peace would restore itself in that place one day.

They reached the rooftops near the workshop and Leynarve guided him down to the street. Vygeas eased himself over waterspouts and levered past windows, following her nimble lead to the cobblestones. His wounds now throbbed. The numbness his fighting body provided had receded. They reached the front door of the workshop— no longer Fhialain's— and Vygeas knocked.

Arthur opened the door, wearing a wide grin. The waves of appreciation surrounded Vygeas as they entered the workshop.

"Ye are a good man, lord assassin." A white-haired woman who worked the loom rose from her stool and clasped his hand in hers. "We found the place on the map hidden in that chest where our master secreted away his wealth," the woman whispered, leaning close. "Och, but ye are wounded again. Where's 'oor healer?" She turned to a boy near her. "Tell Maisie to come bring her kit. She's needed here."

"Please do so quietly," Leynarve spoke behind Vygeas as the woman led them to the back of the workroom. "We are most likely wanted by the caisteal guards."

"Among others," Vygeas added. "May we stay till nightfall?" he asked Arthur, who had not moved from his side.

"Certainly, my lord assassin," Arthur replied.

"Please do not call me that. I shall no longer be an assassin." Vygeas took the small pouch from his belt. Blood had stained it.

"Oh! I had not noticed that injury. When were you stabbed in the belly, V?" Leynarve moved closer running her warm hands across him, searching for the source of bleeding.

"I wasn't hurt there. It's not my blood." Vygeas tipped the contents of the bag into his hand. A severed finger bearing the signet ring of Gille Fhialain lay in his palm. "Proof of a job well done."

Gasps echoed around the room.

Leynarve emitted a shocked scent and stared in horror at the bloodied digit nestled in his palm.

"So, you did it?" Disappointed accusation filled her tone. Her eyes welled then she turned away.

"Leynarve, I didn't kill him," he pleaded to her back.

She stopped mid-stride. "How did you get your proof then?" She spun to face him, her glare hard as flint.

"This man can live without a finger, but I cannot live without his. I will take this to Lord Ciarán, pay my debt, and be released from his service. I survived his assassins. I deserve it."

"So, you saved the man and his family?"

"Aye." His heart quickened at her stare.

Her look was softening. Leynarve then frowned and her lips parted, revealing those two crooked teeth.

"So, our master still lives?" Arthur's words were loud with accusation. "Will he not return and claim back what is his?" He stepped forward.

Leynarve's shoulders tensed at his shout.

"No, Arthur, he will not. His life, and the lives of his family, would be forfeited if he did." Vygeas explained to the gathering crowd of workers. "He knows all is lost here."

Murmurs came from the back of the group, plus a discontentment.

"Your master was a greedy man, but he did not deserve death. Only pointing out of his wrongs. Fhialain will make a fresh start in another place, with a different name where his daughters can grow up in contentment." Vygeas cast a steely frown at the small section of the crowd who emanated the severest annoyance at his revelation. "Would you have the lives of his children taken? For the other assassins visiting this isle would kill those innocents along with their parents."

The loom near the front of the shop ceased its *clanking*. Eyes scoured the floor and shame floated from the group who had spiked irritation moments earlier.

"I think ye are in the wrong profession, my Lord Vygeas." The white-haired woman stated. Agreement rose from all corners of the room.

The workers returned to their tasks in quietness. Perhaps they mulled over the outcome his assistance had produced for them. He was at last alone with Leynarve who stood motionless at the back of the workshop. An aroma of mixed emotions floated from her. It was hard to decipher them all.

"I am a warrior." Vygeas began. *I must explain myself.* "There's a war brewing. Lord Ciarán is evil. He opposes the high king of Dál Gaedhle, the Ard Righ, Donnach MacEnoicht. I shall fight for *him*. For what is right." He leaned his hand on his dagger handle while he shooed away the pain in his wounds and the dark that lurked, threatening to prevent the words from leaving his lips. Words essential for his life to continue with peace and purpose. "Leynarve, I know what I did to your parents was unpardonable. But I am not that man anymore." He swallowed. "And I have promised myself I will never be so again."

The silence stretched. *Oh, please. Let it be that Leynarve would answer me!*

She did not. She did not even lift her eyes from the floor.

"I want to trust you... Can I?" Now she flicked her brown gaze to his face. "You killed the woman you loved."

His heart seized. "Elyse was doomed to a torment that would last forever at the hands of Drostan. I know not how but he *would* have done it. He was in touch with it—*evil*—somehow. He glowed a blackness. I saw it when I returned to him after I received the gifting. He's gone now. That storm was his death throw, and he can threaten your life no longer." He sighed heavily. "I did it out of love, but I know the act itself was wrong. And for many such acts I have damned myself to the place from which I endeavoured to keep Elyse."

The chatter of workers and clattering of looms were soft background noise filling the silence he wished Leynarve would break. But she did not.

"But to love...is that not a noble trait...a start on the path to a redemption of sorts?"

Her lips thinned and she wouldn't meet his eyes.

Very well, I have naught to lose.

"I ask you again, Lady Leynarve of Monsae." Vygeas knelt on one knee before her, his throat threatening to constrict. "Can you forgive me?" He held out his hand to her, beseeching, his senses seeking to understand her perfume.

"I can't...obliterate what you've done." Leynarve replied. "It's part of my history and will always be so." She looked at his hand as she spoke. "But I remind myself, if not you, then another assassin— one not as merciful— would have performed Lord Ciarán's bidding. And completed it in its entirety." The muscles of her slender throat worked. "The consequences of that night set me on a course...a path which led me to you, Vygeas. I cannot alter that which has happened to me and my family. But I *can* change the way I feel about the man who did it. Especially now the man has changed. I can choose to release myself from the hurt I feel and my want for revenge. To be free of it, as a wise lad once explained to me, so it doesn't enslave me."

Vygeas blinked. The thudding in his temples threatened to drown out Leynarve's words.

She spoke of pardon...

"It is something I need to work on..."— she looked him in the eye then— "The letting go. But I find the way I feel about the man is assisting the process. And I know one day, the liking I have will overpower the hating I had...and maybe, if the man wishes, it can become more."

Vygeas let himself breathe again. Warmth filled his chest. The precious warmth of hope. Leynarve smiled at him and reached forward, taking his hand and pulling him to stand.

The front door to the workshop burst open and Aiden ran in from the street.

"My lord?" Aiden yelled, then spying them at the far end of the room, strode by the workers busy at their tasks. "Ye are injured?" The young man's curls bobbed in concern.

Vygeas sighed. The moment of Leyna's openness had dissolved, but the anticipation of continuing with the woman before him lingered. The smart, brave, beautiful, and resourceful Lady Leynarve of Monsae, who had saved his life in many ways.

Vygeas faced his knave, his brow tight.

"Why aren't you holding Dräger?"

EPILOGUE

Bram rapped on the heavy oak door to Lord Ciarán's room in the round tower and straightened his shoulders.

I would stand before this lord and never flinch, no matter the disdain thrown at me.

"Yes?" His master's lord dragged out the word behind the closed door. "Come in, then!"

Bram breathed deep, turned the handle, and pushed open the door.

Lord Ciarán sat at his desk and peered at a parchment in front of him, a bronze statuette of a dragon keeping one edge firmly on the desktop. The sides of the stiff scroll fought against the beast's effigy and strained to return to its original curled position and prevent further inspection by the grey-haired lord who held the other end down with a fist. He lifted his attention from his parchment and placed his scrutiny upon Bram.

"What do you want?" Lord Ciarán's eyes retained their squint.

"My lord, my master Drostan will not be returning."

Lord Ciarán's eyes slitted. "You know this how?"

"I have seen it. He has...left this world, Lord Ciarán." Bram's throat worked past the lump it held.

Lord Ciarán stood, lifting his fist from the parchment. It snapped shut, reverting with speed to its rolled state, skidding the dragon statuette off the desk where it then *thunked* on the floor.

"Are you speaking of his death? Have you seen it?" Lord Ciarán's voice rose, and he moved from his chair. "So, he will not be bringing Lady Leynarve to me?" He stepped around the desk, knocking the dragon sculpture with his slippered foot so it skidded along the wooden floor and crashed against the fire hearth. *"Dragon's breath!"* He limped to the narrow window. "And I am now without a mage."

Lord Ciarán spun, his grey eyes raking Bram from top to toe.

"He's taught you enough. You'll do." He nodded his decision and turned, muttering, "Where would I get another from? Those tight-fisted—"

"I am your mage now, my lord." It was a statement, not a question.

I will let this lord know I am no servant.

"Yes, well, your first task is to aid my search for dragons." Lord Ciarán rubbed his chin, the rasp as his hand ran over stubble was the only sound in the room for some moments. "I must relinquish my quest for Lady Leynarve of Monsae. And his competitors would have dealt with that assassin by now. I have larger armies to acquire, and greater battles lie ahead." His steel-grey eyes bore into Bram's. "Your predecessor investigated the existence of the great beasts, although none have sighted one since the Dragon Wars of millennia past." He huffed. "He has taught you of them?"

Bram nodded in reply with an ache in his heart at this lord's omission of condolence—a non-acknowledgement of the greatness of the sorcerer who now passed from this—

"I need one. Go look in your pot." Lord Ciarán flicked his hand at Bram and turned back to the curled parchment on top of his desk. "You can leave this caisteal without problems, yes? Not tied to stone, or any other element, are you?"

Bram dug his nails into his palms to conquer the burning within himself.

I will endure this man. Lord Ciarán was Drostan's lord, but he will never be mine.

Bram's master—his new master—was one more powerful than this lordling human who stood there, arrogance personified.

Bram would use Lord Ciarán as he could, but he would answer to no man.

His one true ruler, the spirit he met in the cave, had shown him greater realms.

Bram would serve him, and him only.

If you enjoyed this story, please leave a review.

Join Jenn Lees newsletter community for news of new releases and extras.

www.jennleeswriter.com

Acknowledgements

I love fantasy. It's my personal reading choice. For years, even before I started writing, I've had a fantasy story in my head that takes place in a beautiful world—most of it very much like Scotland.

So, I am very excited to bring to you this wee introductory story to the world of Dál Cruinne.

I hope you enjoy the characters and their journey, and you will see them in future novels set in Dál Cruinne. Murtairean is the Gaelic word for assassins.

I'd like to thank our son, Frank, who unknowingly supplied the inspiration for Vygeas' gift of enhanced senses.

Thank you, Annie Seaton, for editing, and for everything else you taught me about self-publishing.

Also, Sally Odgers for a manuscript assessment of the second edition.

Thanks to Melinda Graham, my critique partner, and Jill Williams, Ileana Noble, Sue Jacka, and Graham Shaw, plus Karen Sweet, my beta readers for this story.

Also, the judges of Ink & Insights 2019 who gave me invaluable feedback on the first 10 000 words of an earlier draft and encouraged me to expand my novella into a short novel.

And as always, my husband Frank, thanks for the support and continuing to believe in me.

About the Author

DESTINY RELATIONSHIP COURAGE

DESTINY RELATIONSHIP COURAGE

Retired nurse Jenn has travelled extensively and lived on three continents. Although Australia is the land of her birth, Scotland has always called her back. This country remains her source of inspiration, where she now lives with her husband, and close family nearby.

Jenn loves walking through a forest and climbing a mountain to experience the view. Or exploring a castle ruin and soaking in the history. Her only disappointment in life is that time travel is not possible... apparently.

Award-winning fantasy author Jenn Lees' latest release, *Of High Kings and Mages: Arlan's Pledge Book Three*, reached the Semi-Finalist stage in the OZMA Book Awards for Fantasy Fiction 2024 CIBAs (Chanticleer International Book Awards).

Of Warriors and Sages: Arlan's Pledge Book Two reached Semi-Finalist in the OZMA Book Awards for Fantasy Fiction 2023 (as the manuscript *The Quest*). Longlisted in the Realm Awards 2025 Fantasy Section. As the manuscript *The Quest* reached the Top 10 in Ink & Insights 2021.

Jenn Lees' Best Selling novel, *Of Myths And Portals: Arlan's Pledge Book One* achieved First Place Award (Gold) in The BookFest Fall 2024 Fiction-Romance-Fantasy, Second Place Award (Silver) in The BookFest fall 2024 Fiction-Fantasy-Magic, Myths and Legends, and Fiction-Christian-Fantasy

The Crossing: Arlan's Pledge Book 1 (re-released as *Of Myths and Portals*) achieved the finals in the OZMA Book Awards for Fantasy Fiction (previous draft manuscript) CIBA 2021. *Restoring Time* (Book 4 of the *Community Chronicles Series*) reached the finals in the CYGNUS Awards for Science Fiction 2021 CIBA.

An Ink & Insights Competition judge says of *Arlan's Pledge*:

'Beautifully crafted, full of rich setting descriptions, tension that caught my attention and kept it, and characters that leapt off the page. This author is a skilled storyteller.' (Melody Quinn. Ink & Insights 2021 Competition Master Category Judge)

Find out more about Jenn Lees and her novels.
Sign up for the newsletter and receive *Running with the Stags*, a free novella in the *Arlan's Pledge Series.*
www.jennleeswriter.com
Want more of Jenn Lees?
Support Jenn Lees Fantasy Author on Patreon. https://www.patreon.com/c/jennleesfantasyauthor/members

ALSO BY

ARLAN'S PLEDGE SERIES
OF MYTHS AND PORTALS: ARLAN'S PLEDGE BOOK ONE
Destiny must claim them
(Previously published as *The Crossing: Arlan's Pledge Book One*)
OF WARRIORS AND SAGES: ARLAN'S PLEDGE BOOK TWO.
The heart-quest must win
OF HIGH KINGS AND MAGES: ARLAN'S PLEDGE BOOK THREE
A king must die

THE COMMUNITY CHRONICLES SERIES
The Crash: Community Chronicles Book 1 An introductory Novella.
Stolen Time: Community Chronicles Book 2
Saving Time: Community Chronicles Book 3
Restoring Time: Community Chronicles Book 4

All Jenn's novels are also available in eBook and audiobook